To all my friends at
Focus on the Family Publishing.
Thanks for all you do to make it possible
for Sierra and Christy to spend time with
each other and with all their real-life
friends around the world.

Chapter One

S IERRA'S HEART POUNDED. HER PULSE HAMMERED
in her ears. Gripping the armrests of her seat, she
tried to scream, but no sound emerged.

*We're going to crash! This airplane is about to nosedive
into the freezing Atlantic Ocean! We're doomed!*

Instead of Sierra's whole life passing before her eyes,
only the events of the past few days flashed through her
mind. She saw herself at Doug and Tracy's wedding in
Southern California. Her sister, Tawni, was catching the
bouquet. Her good friend Christy was standing beside
Aunt Marti, and all of a sudden they were inviting Sierra
to go with the two of them to Switzerland.

Then Sierra saw herself in California, prompting her
parents over the phone as they searched her messy room
in Portland to find her passport. "Try looking on my
desk," she urged them. "Or maybe it's in the bottom
dresser drawer."

These suggestions drifted from Sierra as she watched
herself boarding a plane early that morning with her
passport in hand.

Now, here she was, spiraling into the icy blue. Sierra screamed inside her mind.

From far away, a familiar voice called, "Sierra, are you okay?"

She felt a soft touch on her rigid arm. The voice seemed to come closer. Sierra's eyes fluttered open, and she gasped for breath.

"We're getting ready to land," Christy said from the seat beside Sierra. "Are you okay? You were talking in your sleep."

Sierra blinked at Christy and took in her surroundings. Looking out the window, she could see the bright blue sky. The plane was confident and steady. In the seats beside Sierra, Christy and Marti were calmly preparing for the landing.

"That was an awful nightmare!" Sierra said, moistening her lips and catching her breath. "I thought we were going to crash." She tried to act as if the idea were funny, but the terror of her dream still loomed over her. The details were too close to reality.

Sierra was actually on a plane headed for Germany. From there, she, Christy, and Marti would take a train into Switzerland. It really had been only a few frenzied days since Sierra had attended Doug and Tracy's wedding in Newport Beach. After the wedding, Sierra had been invited to travel with Christy and Marti at the last minute. Only one part of Sierra's dream wasn't true—the plane showed no signs of spiraling into the Atlantic.

"Do you want a washcloth?" Christy asked. "I took one for you when they came by a little earlier. It's probably cold now."

Sierra opened the cooled cloth and held it over her face, breathing in the faint citrus fragrance. Lifting her long, curly blond hair, she held the washcloth against the back of her neck and looked down at her loose jeans. The mustard stain above her right knee was still there in the shape of an ivy leaf, left over from a deli sandwich she had eaten somewhere above Nova Scotia. When Sierra had tried to open a mustard packet with her teeth, a flying blob had landed on her leg. She rubbed at the stain with the washcloth. It didn't help. The spot would probably be with her for the rest of the trip.

Because Sierra, Christy, and Aunt Marti had left for Europe from Marti's house in Southern California, Sierra hadn't gone home to Portland to pack the right kind of clothes for Switzerland in August. She also hadn't been able to help her frantic parents when they couldn't find her passport. Fortunately, her brother Gavin had located it behind the dresser, and Mr. and Mrs. Jensen had sent it to Sierra through an overnight delivery service. Now Sierra wished she would have had them send a few more things, like a second pair of jeans.

All the planning had happened so fast. Sierra's parents had been supportive when she called them and explained the invitation to join Christy and Aunt Marti. The Jensens were flexible, and since Sierra was the fourth of six children, they tended to be fairly relaxed about her adventures. But this time, even Sierra wasn't sure what she had gotten herself into.

Christy pulled her shoulder-length nutmeg hair up in a

ponytail holder and crossed her long, slender legs. Sierra noticed that Christy also looked a little uneasy. Maybe she was stiff from sitting on the plane for 12 hours. Or maybe Aunt Marti was getting under Christy's skin the way Marti had already irritated Sierra.

"What time will it be when we land?" Sierra asked, adjusting her seat belt.

"Eight twenty-seven," answered Marti. "Remember, it's morning here. We'll have only an hour to make it through customs, retrieve our luggage, and catch our train to Basel. We need to be quick about this."

Marti meant business—all the time. Sierra wasn't exactly fond of this petite, polished, and pushy woman. Marti had helped Sierra's sister, Tawni, find a modeling job in Southern California, which made Sierra's parents feel more comfortable about Sierra accepting this last-minute ticket to Europe. From anyone else, such an extravagance might be unusual, but with Aunt Marti, money was only a method to accomplish her goals. And right now, it was Marti's goal to get Christy to Switzerland so she could check out a college where she had been offered a scholarship.

"Here," Marti said, opening her leather purse and handing Sierra and Christy a pack of gum. "Start to clear your ears now. We're beginning to descend."

"I don't need a whole pack," Sierra said. "I only want half a stick."

Irritation showed on Marti's perfectly made-up face. Not a hair was out of place, and her knit pantsuit didn't show one wrinkle. How did she manage to look so good after this long flight?

Christy's clear blue-green eyes shot a message to Sierra to take the gum and hush up about it.

"Maybe I'll keep the rest for later," Sierra added quickly. "Thanks."

She stuck half a stick of the winter-green-flavored gum into her mouth and pondered the mystery of why she had been invited on this trip. All Sierra could explain to her parents was that Marti had three ticket vouchers. The third was supposed to be for Christy's boyfriend, Todd, but he couldn't take the time off work to come. Christy's best friend, Katie, had broken her foot only a few days before. Marti hadn't even mentioned bringing her husband, Bob, which Sierra thought was strange. And Christy said her mom turned down the opportunity because she didn't know how she would handle such a long flight.

That left Sierra. She didn't mind being last choice, though. She was excited about the chance to do some more traveling.

"Do you feel rested at all?" Christy asked.

"A little. How about you?"

"I slept for about two hours, I think. Remember how hard it was to get over jet lag when we went to England last January?"

"I remember," Sierra said. "They say it's better if you stay awake the whole first day so you'll be able to sleep that night."

"That's exactly what we're going to do," Marti said, her dark eyes checking Sierra's and Christy's seat belts to make sure they were fastened. "We'll take a train directly from the airport to Basel. After we check into the hotel, I've made an appointment for us to meet with the director of the school at two-thirty this afternoon." She chewed her piece of gum demurely.

"That doesn't give us much time," Christy said. "I mean, for any goof-ups."

Marti gave her a long, raised-eyebrow stare. "We aren't planning on having any 'goof-ups.' And do chew your gum with your lips together, dear."

"I'm just saying I've done a little bit of train travel in Europe before and—"

"—and I haven't?" Marti questioned.

"I didn't hear lunch mentioned in the schedule," Sierra jumped in, hoping to lighten the tone. "When do we eat?"

"We'll eat on the train," Marti said firmly. "At least we're in first class this time."

Sierra knew Marti was still miffed that their airplane seats hadn't been in first class as she had expected. Marti had angrily confronted the clerk at the check-in desk, but the best the airline could do was guarantee Marti first-class seats on the way home.

"It looks as if it's going to be a nice, clear day," Christy said, nodding at the buildings, highways, and fields rapidly becoming visible out their window. "It all seems so charming from up here. Really clean and quaint."

"You don't think it's really like that?" Sierra asked.

She noticed the runway coming into view.

"Well, I've never seen Germany or Switzerland. But some parts of France and Spain weren't exactly postcard settings."

Just as Christy finished her sentence, the plane's tires bumped gently onto the runway, and the giant aircraft slowed.

Sierra gripped her armrests and clenched her teeth, waiting for the plane to stop. *We didn't crash,* she thought. *We're here! It was only a dumb nightmare I probably got from rushing around to get ready for the trip. Or maybe from the pickles on that deli sandwich.*

"Ready? Don't forget your backpacks," Marti urged.

Sierra and Christy exchanged glances as they undid their seat belts and reached for their packs under the seats in front of them. Sierra couldn't help but wonder if Christy was having the same thought she was: A week with Marti might be harder than they realized.

Chapter Two

O MARTI'S DELIGHT, THE TRIP THROUGH customs and the baggage claim went off without a hitch. The women boarded the train, found their reserved spots in a first-class compartment, and flopped into the high-backed seats with sighs of relief.

"I think we set a new traveling record," Christy said.

Marti looked pleased. "This proves my point, ladies. As long as we stay together and stay organized, we can stay on schedule."

"I'm starving," Sierra said, sliding her pack onto the overhead shelf. "Anyone else ready to head to the dining car with me?"

"They come to us here in first class," Marti said, settling back into the seat and glancing out the window as the train began to pull out of the station.

Sierra looked at Christy and back at Marti. "Would you mind if I went ahead and got something in the dining car or at the snack bar? I'm seriously starving." The truth was Sierra's stomach had turned into a big, churning bubble. She wasn't sure if it was the flight or the nerve-wracking nightmare, but she knew a glass of milk would help.

"Oh, go ahead," Marti said. "Both of you. Just stay together and don't talk to strangers. Here's some money."

"Would you like us to bring anything back for you?" Christy asked.

"No, I'll wait. Thank you."

Sliding open the compartment door, Sierra stepped into the narrow hallway with Christy right behind her. They made their way single file toward the dining car. As the train picked up speed, it swayed gently from side to side. They opened the door into the next car and continued their journey until they reached the dining section. Sierra entered first and slid into the upholstered bench seat of the first open table she saw. A white cloth covered the table, and a short vase by the window held a yellow rosebud, which seemed to nod its head at them in greeting.

Christy sat across from Sierra. "How are you doing?" she asked, leaning closer.

"My stomach is a mess," Sierra admitted. "I think I'll be fine once I eat something, though. How are you doing?"

"Pretty good. Has my aunt driven you completely crazy yet?"

"Not yet." Sierra looked above Christy's head as a tall man in a gray sweatshirt approached them. At first, Sierra thought he might be the waiter, but then she realized he was dressed too casually.

To her surprise, he stopped at their table and with a polite nod asked, *"Sprechen Sie Deutsch?"*

Christy shook her head. "We're Americans," she answered.

"Ah!" He said, his gaze on Sierra. "Of course you are. Americans. Very nice."

His accent was charming, his expression gentle. All of a sudden, Sierra felt she really *was* on the other side of the world.

"I think perhaps I have left a parcel on your seat."

Sierra looked down, and there, next to the window, was a small package wrapped with brown paper and tied with string.

"Here it is," she said, handing it to him.

The man touched his heart with his hand. "Thank God. It is my gift for my friends. I am on holiday. And you?"

Christy and Sierra looked at each other. Neither spoke up right away.

"Oh, I am sorry," he said, reading their expressions. "I have interrupted something. I can leave if you would like."

"That's okay," Sierra heard herself say. "We just arrived this morning, and we're not quite adjusted to the time and everything yet." She felt Christy give her a little kick under the table.

The man looked harmless enough, in Sierra's opinion. His face was long with high cheekbones and a narrow chin. He wore his dark hair smoothed straight back except for a resistant strand that hung like a black crescent moon over his right eye. His eyes were dark but clear and alive—full of intrigue.

"I am called Alexander," he said, extending his hand to Sierra.

She placed her small hand in his and received his firm, decisive shake.

"My name is Sierra."

"Sa-har-a?" he repeated. "Like the desert?"

"No, *Sierra*. Like the mountains in California."

"You are named for mountains in California?" Alexander asked.

"Sort of. I used to live in the mountains. Now I live in the city—in Portland. That's in Oregon. Do you know where that is?"

"Of course, yes. And you?" he asked, turning to Christy.

Christy hesitated for a moment. "I'm Christy."

"Christy," he repeated. The "r" rolled off his tongue beautifully. "You are also from rainy Portland?" Alexander asked.

"You've definitely heard about Portland," Sierra said.

She smiled at Alexander and then at Christy, hoping her friend would lighten up. But Christy pursed her lips together and looked down at her hands. Sierra wondered if Christy was remembering Aunt Marti's warning about not talking to strangers. But they were in Europe. People were friendly like this on the trains. What could happen to the two of them? Alexander seemed harmless enough to Sierra. Harmless and intriguing.

"Actually, I live in California," Christy said after an uncomfortable pause.

The waiter stepped up to their table and asked in German what they would like.

"Allow me," Alexander said. He spoke in a deep, rumbling tone, first to the waiter, then to Sierra and Christy. "Did you wish to order some breakfast?" Alex asked them.

"We just wanted a sandwich or something," Sierra said. "And some milk."

Alex spoke again to the waiter and then, nodding his head, said, *"Danke."*

Sierra moved closer to the window, making room for Alex to sit down. "Would you like to join us?"

"If this would be all right with you both, then yes." Alex sat down next to Sierra.

She noticed his gray sweatshirt was made from a heavy woven fabric. It didn't look like the thick cotton knits available in the States.

"Are you from around here?" Sierra asked, deciding that she might as well be the one to ask questions.

"I am on holiday to see friends in Basel. This is where my mother is from. I have many relatives here. My father is from Russia. I have been seven years living in Moscow. I lived in Basel before that time." Alexander leaned back and looked at Sierra with his gentle smile. "If you live in two different states, how did you then come to be friends?"

"We met in England last January on a . . . " Sierra

thought a moment before answering. "We're Christians," she blurted out. "We were on a missions trip."

A warm smile spread across Alexander's strong face. A friendly chuckle emerged from his lips. "You will not believe," Alexander said, laughing. "I am also Christian. Four years now."

Sierra felt relieved and delighted at the same time. She and Christy both laughed in camaraderie with Alexander.

"We would call this a God-thing, Alexander," Christy said.

"Yes! Please. Call me Alex. Yes, this is good. You being Christian makes for easier conversation, no?"

"Yes," Sierra agreed. She was glad to see that Christy had relaxed and that they didn't have to feel uneasy about Alex. Sierra liked the feeling that had come over the three of them. In the past she had discovered that when she was away from home and out of her familiar routine, she learned to trust God more. She had seen Him provide for and protect her many times in situations in which she was out of her element. Now God had provided another Christian for her and Christy to share their first meal with in Germany.

The server stood at their table, swaying slightly with the train's rhythm. He carefully placed before them a basket of hard, crusted rolls, a plate of thinly sliced ham and cheese, and a bowl of individually wrapped butters and jellies. They each received a small silver pot of coffee, and a pitcher of milk was placed before Sierra.

"This is what you ordered?" she asked.

"Yes." Alex looked concerned. "Is it not what you wanted? Did you not say milk for your coffee?"

"This is fine," Christy said quickly.

"It's fine. Really," Sierra said. She wondered if it would be tacky to pour the milk directly into her coffee cup and drink it all.

"I must tell you something," Alex said, pouring his coffee and looking long at Sierra. "There is a beautiful innocence about you. About both of you. It is as if I am gazing on the first tulips of spring."

Then, because she couldn't help it, Sierra burst out laughing. She wondered if her forehead had an invisible sign emblazoned on it that said "Sweet 16 and never been kissed."

"Did I say something not correct?" Alex looked at Christy.

"It was sweet of you to say that. I guess we just didn't expect it," Christy responded.

Sierra checked herself. "Are you always this intense with people you've just met?"

"Yes," Alex said, looking serious.

Sierra swallowed her laughter. "I bet you are. You'll have to excuse me for laughing. I'm not used to guys like you."

"And I am not used to girls like you. This is a good compliment."

Sierra took a sip of her coffee. It was one part coffee and 10 parts milk.

"You two must have boyfriends who wait in long lines

for you. Do they do this—make long lines in front of your houses?"

It was all Sierra could do not to spew her coffee mixture when Alex said that. She quickly swallowed the murky, lukewarm beverage and said, "Christy has found her true love. I'm still interviewing all the guys in my long line."

Alex sat up a little straighter and tilted his chin. He flipped back the lock of dark hair that hung over his eye. "Then I should like to get in line. I am ready for interview. First question, please."

Sierra had never felt so charmed. She put her hand over her mouth to keep from laughing. "Okay. Here's your first question." She picked up one of the tiny containers next to the jelly. "What is this?"

"Oh, how do you call it? Ah . . . I do not know this in English."

Sierra shook her head and, with a "tsk, tsk," said, "I'm sorry. You'll have to go to the back of the line."

Alex laughed and then said, "You must try it. You will know it. Take some on the bread."

Both Sierra and Christy tried some.

"It's kind of like cream cheese," Christy said.

"Cream cheese," Alex repeated. "Yes, cream cheese. Now do I get to ask you a question?"

Sierra licked the last dab of the sweet cream cheese from her lip. "Sure. Ask me a question."

"How do you make your hair so?"

"So . . . what?" Sierra asked.

"I have never seen hair so . . . so beautiful."

Sierra shook her head again. This time she looked at Christy and said, "Some guys will say anything to get to the front of the line."

Chapter Three

"**M**ARTI?" SIERRA SLID OPEN THE DOOR TO their train compartment, and tall Alex ducked to enter with Sierra and Christy. "Marti, this is Alex."

"I am pleased to meet you," Alex said, extending a hand to Marti.

She ignored him. "Where did you meet this young man?" Marti asked the girls.

"In the dining car," Sierra said innocently. "We had breakfast together."

Marti looked shocked. Alex withdrew his hand.

"I do not mean to interrupt here. I will go. It was my pleasure to meet you, See-hair-a." He reached for her hand; but instead of shaking it, he held it warmly.

"And to meet you, Christy." Alex kept hold of Sierra's hand and nodded at Christy. "Perhaps we will meet again soon."

"It isn't likely," Marti said coolly.

Alex smiled. He slowly released Sierra's hand, gave a pleasant nod to all of them, and left.

"You didn't have to scare him off," Sierra said, lowering herself onto the seat across from Marti. Her right hand still felt the warmth of Alex's touch.

Marti's dark eyes blazed as she looked incredulously at Sierra. "Excuse me? I tell you and Christy not to talk to strangers, and you come back with some scruffy German boy and expect me to be delighted with your behavior?"

"He's not German. He's Russian," Sierra said under her breath.

"Russian!" Marti looked shocked. "What in the world are you doing speaking with a Russian?"

"Aunt Marti," Christy said calmly, "I know it seems as though we went against your wishes, but we didn't. We just happened to meet Alex in the dining car. He left his package on the seat."

"That was convenient," Marti said.

"No, it wasn't like that. He's a very nice person. He's a Christian. We felt totally comfortable around him. You would like him if you gave him a chance. Nothing was against your instructions, really," Christy responded.

"I told you not to speak to strangers. You deliberately went against my instructions. What kind of a trip will this be if you two don't follow my wishes?"

Sierra bit her lip to keep from saying anything.

Christy sat on the upholstered bench seat next to Sierra. "Look, Aunt Marti, we both appreciate your taking us on this trip, but the fact is, I'm 19 years old, and I've traveled halfway across Europe by myself on a train. I think you know you can trust me. This whole trip is going to be really frustrating for all of us unless you treat Sierra and me like responsible adults."

"I'll treat you like adults when you begin to act like adults. Starting up conversations with Russians is not the way to prove you're responsible."

"He's only half Russian," Christy stated. "His mother is Swiss, and he grew up in Basel."

"And that's supposed to make everything all right?" Marti said. "I don't want you two consorting with strangers. Is that clear?"

Christy and Sierra looked at each other and then nodded.

"Yes," Christy said. "We'll go by your rules."

She leaned back, let out a long huff, and folded her arms across her chest. Sierra looked over and noticed Christy had closed her eyes. It seemed to be the only way to block out Marti's railings. Sierra followed Christy's lead and did the same.

Alexander. . . . Why did Marti have to scare him off? I want to see him again. There's something special about him. I'm sure we'll see him when we get off the train. He's going to Basel, too. And we told him where we were staying. He'll come find me. I know he will. Sierra smiled to herself.

"When is that cart coming by?" Marti asked. "I'm awfully hungry. The service in these countries is nothing like it is at home. It's disgraceful, really."

"We can get you something," Christy offered.

"Don't think I don't know what you're trying to do, Christina. No, you may not sneak out to meet your foreign friend. Consider yourself grounded to this compartment. Both of you."

Sierra couldn't imagine how humiliated Christy probably felt. It was bad enough to be grounded in the first place, but even worse in front of Sierra—especially when Christy was only trying to be nice.

The train began to slow. Sierra gazed out the window as they pulled into a station, but she didn't catch the name of the town on a sign they rolled past. Several rows of track were laid on either side of the covered station, and dozens of travelers hurried across the landings. Large billboards advertised soft drinks, chocolates, and cigarettes—all in German, of course. Sierra tried to break down the words to see if she could decode any of them. It made her wish she knew more languages. She had taken Spanish during her first two years in high school, but she didn't know if she would be able to converse in Spanish if the need arose. It amazed her that Alex spoke several languages and that his English was still very good. He was such a gentle-spirited guy.

Just then the door to their compartment opened, and Sierra looked up, hoping that Alex had been bold enough to return in spite of Marti. A gray-haired gentleman in a suit entered, carrying a black briefcase. He checked his train ticket for the seat number and then tucked it into his coat pocket, greeting them in German.

Marti put on a tight smile and looked him over.

His eyes moved around the room, politely acknowl-edging the three of them. He spoke to Marti again in

German, motioning toward her seat by the window. She didn't answer him.

"I think you're in his seat," Sierra said.

"Just so," the man said. He had switched to English. "That is my seat number, but it does not matter to me. Please. I'll sit here."

Marti offered him an obligatory nod.

"You are, I suppose, three sisters traveling together?" he said as he settled into the seat.

"Oh, no," Marti said, suddenly coming alive with a ripple of laughter. "This is my niece and her friend. We're not sisters."

"You certainly look like three sisters to me," the man said. His voice was smooth, the look in his eye was keen, and his aftershave was strong enough to be considered an air freshener back in the States.

Oh, brother! Sierra rolled her eyes. *Does this guy think he is suave, or what? I can't believe Marti is actually flirting with him. At least Christy and I weren't flirting with Alex. We had a much deeper conversation. How can Marti judge us when she acts worse than we do around strangers?*

"We're on our way to Basel," Marti said. "Perhaps you can suggest a good restaurant. I'm afraid the cart hasn't found its way back here yet, and we're all very hungry."

"The service is not always what it should be on this part of the trip. I was going to get myself a cup of coffee," the man said. "May I bring back enough for all of us?"

"None for me," Christy said.

"Nothing for me," Sierra added.

"That would be very nice of you . . . " Marti paused, waiting for the man to give his name.

"Gernot," he volunteered. "And you are?"

"Marti," she said slowly, as if he wouldn't understand her unless she exaggerated her words.

Before Gernot could rise to get the coffees, the cart and attendant appeared at the door. Gernot insisted he buy the coffee and roll for Marti and even bought chocolate bars for all of them. For the next hour, Sierra pretended to be asleep. Actually, she did doze off and on, but it was hard not to stay awake listening to the spicy conversation between Gernot and Marti.

This is weird. Really weird, Sierra thought. *First, Christy and I get grounded for our innocent conversation over breakfast with Alex—and now we're locked in this compartment, listening to a middle-aged, married woman carry on a flirting fest with a smooth talker who is wearing smelly aftershave.*

Feeling nervous about what might happen next, Sierra could only imagine what Christy was thinking and feeling. Sierra couldn't wait for the train to stop so she and Christy could talk all this over. They had to be almost to Basel by now.

Staring out the window, Sierra saw rolling green hills dotted with old, timber-framed farmhouses. A forest of towering evergreens covered the rise to the south. She decided that must be the Black Forest, which meant they were close to Basel, since it was located just over the border from the Black Forest.

She wondered if Alex was looking out his window right now, too. Was he on the same side of the train? Was he seeing the same beautiful hills and thinking of her the way she was thinking of him?

Sierra mentally went over their conversation at breakfast after they had quit joking with each other. Alex had said that he'd studied on his own to improve his English and then taught himself French. He also spoke Russian, German, and some Italian. He had already finished school but was hoping to be accepted at a university where he would study economics. Sierra sighed. Alex seemed so intelligent and fun at the same time.

The peaceful scenery rolled past. Sierra eyed green grass, cows grazing on the hillsides, and tumbling brambles of wild berries. Children in shorts played in front of houses with red tile roofs. Everything seemed perfect in the scenic world outside.

Sierra couldn't help but think that if she could see Alex one more time, everything in her world would be perfect, too.

Chapter Four

IGHT BEFORE THEY ARRIVED IN BASEL, sweet-smelling Gernot offered to drive Marti and the girls to their hotel and treat them to lunch at his favorite bistro. Marti declined, explaining they already had plans. Until that point, she had chatted happily with Gernot. But when he made the offer, Marti backed off in a hurry. Gernot still lingered at the Basel station, making sure they had all their luggage and knew which direction to go.

Marti thanked him and took off, walking with purpose across the long, crowded platform. Sierra did her best to follow Marti, but she kept turning to look for Alex. Any sign of him and Sierra was sure her heart would jump into her throat. She'd be happy with just one more smile and a wave from him.

Alexander didn't appear—not on the platform, not inside the train station, not in the line at customs, and not on the street where they caught a taxi to the hotel. Gernot seemed to have disappeared, too.

From the backseat of the taxi, Sierra took one last

look over her shoulder, scanning the stream of visitors coming and going from the Basel station. She saw no sign of Alex.

"He'll probably call the hotel," Christy whispered, leaning over and invading Sierra's thoughts.

"Am I that obvious?" Sierra asked.

"He really liked you, didn't he?" Christy said.

Sierra smiled timidly.

"He knows where we're staying and what our plans are for the rest of the week. He'll call. You'll see," Christy comforted Sierra.

The taxi slowed and stopped only a few miles from the train station.

"You want *how* much?" Marti said when they climbed out. Sierra and Christy gathered their luggage as Marti counted out the money.

Twenty minutes later in their hotel rooms, she was still muttering about the cab. "I've never paid so much for a cab!" She checked her watch and motioned for the girls to go to their room through the common door. "We have only 45 minutes before we meet the school's director. You two hurry and get ready. I'm going to freshen up now."

Sierra stretched out on the wide bed with the fluffy, white comforter. "Freshen up? I'd rather take a nap."

"No," Christy said. "We have to stay awake, remember? Maybe you should try to wake yourself up with a quick shower."

"You go ahead. I'll just take a little cat nap."

Christy jumped into the shower, and Sierra floated on

her cloudlike bed. She remembered how good it felt to have Alex look at her with such admiration and how warm his hand felt as it covered hers.

"You're next," Christy said, tapping Sierra's foot and interrupting her dream.

"And you're cruel. I was about to get to the good part of my dream." Sierra rolled over, snatched a pillow, and, through bleary eyes, tossed it at Christy.

"You missed. Come on. The shower felt great, and clean clothes are going to feel even better."

Sierra dramatically peeled herself off the bed and staggered toward the bathroom. "I'm never going to make it."

"Sure you will. And if you know what's good for you, you'll be ready in five minutes."

"Right."

Sierra forced herself to snap out of her drowsy state. The last thing she needed was to invoke Marti's wrath. Sierra's shower in the blue-and-white-tiled stall was speedy, mostly because she didn't wash her hair. It was easier to pull back her mane than to wash and try to tame it. She smiled, remembering how Alex had said she had beautiful hair. He was a unique guy. Sierra turned to face the water, letting it pour over her face. When she finished her shower, she did feel better. Christy was right.

Pulling on a pair of clean shorts and a knit shirt, Sierra opened the bathroom door with a grand "Ta-da!"

Christy stood in the middle of their small room wearing a dress and trying to towel-dry her hair.

"Don't tell me I'm supposed to wear a dress," Sierra said.

"I'm sure it doesn't matter what you wear. I just know how my aunt expects me to dress. You're fine."

"This time, maybe," Sierra said, tossing her dirty clothes over the back of the chair next to the writing desk. "But if we go anywhere that requires nice clothes, I don't have anything with me. Not even my gauze skirt. It ripped. Remember? That's why I borrowed your yellow dress for Doug and Tracy's wedding."

"Don't worry about it. You look fine. I'm sure we'll manage to do some shopping before we leave Basel." Christy rummaged through her backpack and pulled out a small, over-the-shoulder leather purse. "Do you have your passport and everything? The school is back over the border in the Black Forest. We'll probably need our passports."

"I'll get mine," Sierra said.

Marti's long fingernails tapped on their common door. Sierra reached for her leather slip-on shoes and grabbed her backpack.

"Ready, girls?" Aunt Marti called out, then opened the door. A pouf of strong fragrance rushed in ahead of her. "Sierra, you're not dressed yet."

"I told her what she had on was okay," Christy said quickly. "She doesn't have anything but shorts and jeans. We need to go shopping while we're here."

Marti seemed to brighten. "That's a marvelous idea. Perhaps we can squeeze in a few shops on our way back this afternoon."

Sierra made a mental note. *When in doubt, tell Marti you want to go shopping.*

"Christy," Marti said, turning her attention to her dutiful niece, "you're not going with wet hair, are you?"

"It'll dry on the way," Christy said, heading for the door. "I have our room key, Sierra."

Marti and Sierra followed Christy to the elevator.

"This is a nice hotel," Christy commented as they waited for the elevator to reach their third floor.

"It's not bad," Marti said. "Rather plain but clean. Efficient, like so many of these European places. But for the price I'm paying, I expected larger rooms at least."

"I think it's fine," Christy said. She flipped back her hair, and Marti looked put out.

"You girls and your long hair. I can't believe you're going out with it sopping wet. What is taking this elevator so long?" Marti tapped her foot impatiently.

Just then the bell above the door rang, and the doors opened. There stood Alex.

"Hello! I was coming to see you," he said.

Sierra smiled at Alex, then glanced at Marti. Sierra noticed Marti's face turning a shade of burgundy.

"That was very nice of you, but we must leave. We are in a hurry." Marti brushed past Alex and entered the elevator, where she pushed the button for the lobby. "Come, girls."

"Hi," Sierra said softly as she moved past Alex. He reached over, and his fingers touched hers for the briefest moment.

"Sorry, Alex. We're on our way out," Christy offered, trying to smooth things over.

"Yes, to the Schwarzwald Volkschule—I mean, the Black Forest People's School. My cousin has lent me his car for the afternoon. I thought I would drive you," Alex said. He stood outside the elevator while the three women remained inside.

Marti slapped her hand on the button to close the elevator door. "No, thank you," she said firmly, not looking at Alex as the doors closed.

Sierra turned from Marti and, in disbelief at what was happening, looked at Alex. "I'm sorry," she said as the doors clanged shut and the lift took them rapidly down.

"You're sorry?" Marti looked at Sierra in shock. "Sorry for what? Sorry that you told a complete stranger where we were going? Yes, you *should* be sorry. I can't believe you girls were so foolish!

"And you," Marti said, turning to Christy and pointing a long finger at her. "You know better than to do such a thing. Why didn't you stop your young friend here from divulging all our private plans?"

"I was the one who told him where we were going," Christy said firmly. "You're not being fair, Aunt Marti. Alex is a very nice guy. He's only trying to help. You even said the taxis are far too expensive. How else are we going to get there?"

"We shall take a cab, of course. One can never put a price tag on safety. Accepting rides from complete strangers while we're halfway around the world would be foolish. Now, if Alex is in the lobby when these doors open, I want you both to ignore him. If he persists, I shall notify the hotel management." Marti let out a huff as the doors opened.

Alex was nowhere to be seen. Sierra was glad for his sake. She feared what might have happened to him if Marti reported him. At the same time, Sierra felt sorry for herself. She was sure Alex wouldn't have the guts to show up again and risk offending Marti a third time. Sierra would probably never see him again. Unless . . .

No. Sierra shook the thought from her mind. It wouldn't be right to sneak out to meet Alex somewhere. It was obvious, however, that he wanted to see her again. He had flirted with her, letting his fingers brush against hers. It had felt wonderful.

Maybe I could sneak down to the hotel lobby tonight and somehow get a message to him to meet me there, Sierra schemed. *We could stay in the lobby—it wouldn't exactly be the same as sneaking out.*

Before she got too carried away, Sierra reminded herself that she was Marti's guest. Sierra's parents had given her "the talk" on the phone before she came, reminding her to be honest and respectful to Marti. Mr. and Mrs. Jensen had said, "We expect you to respond to Marti the same way you would to us when it comes to making decisions. This is not a time for you to test your independence, Sierra."

Yeah, but if my parents were here, they wouldn't mind. They would like Alex, Sierra rationalized.

Marti flagged a cab, and she, Christy, and Sierra rode the 12 miles to the Schwarzwald Volkschule in silence. Sierra's heart and head were anything but silent, though. Why should she have to follow the rules if the person she was supposed to obey and respect wasn't being fair?

Sierra was sure that if she were traveling with her mom instead of Marti, this whole embarrassing mess never would have happened. Mrs. Jensen would have liked Alex immediately. Sierra just knew her mom would understand if she had to bend the rules a pinch to get around Marti, the tyrant. That is, if Sierra ever had the opportunity to bend those rules.

Her mind spun with possibilities. She and Christy did have a separate room. Maybe Alex would try calling. He wouldn't give up so easily. And Christy would have to be on Sierra's side. Quickly, Sierra concocted a plan. It was risky, but she had to take some chances.

She had to see Alex one more time.

Chapter Five

"**A**ND THIS IS THE COMPUTER ROOM," SAID Mr. Pratt, the school's director, as he completed the tour of the Schwarzwald Volkschule. He was a large, friendly man, and Sierra liked him the moment they met. She had a feeling Christy liked him, too, which was good. First impressions counted, especially when Christy needed to make a decision quickly. And the fact that Mr. Pratt was so likable probably made Christy feel better about the school.

"All assignments are to be turned in on disk. Those students who have laptops, of course, prefer to use those, but our equipment is available to all the students," Mr. Pratt continued.

"Very impressive," Marti said, admiring the rows of tables laden with computers. "This certainly is a fine institution. I must admit I didn't expect everything to be so modern."

"Well, Europe has been a bit slow to adopt the idea of individuals owning computers, but our school has been blessed with several generous donors who are very committed to keeping us state of the art and accomplishing our educational goals. We offer accredited college courses and require a hands-on practicum." Mr. Pratt checked his watch. "Please excuse me. I was expecting another guest this afternoon. He might be waiting in my office."

"We won't keep you," Marti said. "You've been gracious to allow us this much of your time. Although I'm sure Christy will be eager to see the dormitory situation. May we schedule another appointment to tour the dormitory?"

"We can do that right now, if it's convenient for you. Let me stop by my office a moment on the way out." Mr. Pratt turned off the lights and led them down the long, quiet hallway.

"How many students will be starting here in the fall?" Christy asked.

"We currently have close to 800 registered. That is the most we've ever had. Of course, for many of them, this center is only a place to keep their files."

"What do you mean?" Marti asked.

"We have several schools, which we call 'on location.' The students are registered here, but all the course work and professors are at various ends of the earth. For instance, we have 50 students enrolled in Israel and nearly 100 who will study anthropology in Australia. Over a third of our student body studies on location."

"I didn't realize that," Christy said. "Can you tell me about the orphanage in Basel?"

"Yes, of course. You will be going there tomorrow, won't you? I believe they're expecting you at ten o'clock." Mr. Pratt opened the door to his brightly painted office and invited them inside.

"We'll need directions to give the cab driver," Marti said, stepping into the room.

Out of the corner of her eye, Sierra noticed someone sitting on the sofa against the wall. The person stood to greet them.

"Or I could drive you," the deep voice said.

"Alexander!" Mr. Pratt exclaimed. He rushed forward and began to speak to Alex in rapid German. The two exchanged warm greetings.

Sierra felt her heart flutter. She quickly turned to catch Marti's shocked expression.

"Please excuse me," Mr. Pratt said. "I haven't seen this young man for several years. He's been living in Moscow. Alex, I'd like you to meet—"

Before Mr. Pratt could finish the introduction, Alex interrupted him. "We've already met," he said, his eyes fixed on Sierra. "Perhaps you can give Christy's aunt some comfort. Let her know I am not such a strange person."

"Oh, I never . . . ," Marti fumbled. "I mean, it was a strange situation, that's all. One can never be too safe these days, you know."

"I can assure you," Mr. Pratt said with an arm around Alex, "this young man is upright and dependable. You have no cause for concern regarding him. As a matter of fact, let's take a tour of the dormitory, and then you ladies can join us for coffee."

"Oh, that's quite all right," Marti said. "It isn't necessary."

"I insist," Mr. Pratt replied. "I'd like you to be my guests."

"Thank you," Christy said.

At least one of them was thinking clearly enough to respond graciously to Mr. Pratt's invitation. Sierra was too happy to even talk. She couldn't contain her smile.

Alex looked pleased, too. He casually fell into step beside Sierra as they marched down the halls, went out the school's front door, and walked across the street to the dormitory. Mr. Pratt explained that it was one of five large houses run by the school. Students ate together in the main dining room and, every Saturday morning, each student was expected to assist in chores around the house.

As they took the tour, Alex stayed by Sierra's side, taking his own tour of her life. The two of them hung back slightly from the others as Alex asked questions about Sierra's family, her school, her job at Mama Bear's Bakery, and her "hobbits."

"My hobbits?" Sierra asked with a giggle.

"What you like to do for fun," Alex explained. "For example, do you ski?"

"Yes."

"That is your hobbit, then."

"You mean my 'hobby.' Yes, skiing is kind of a hobby for me. Actually, I like most sports, thanks to my dad and my four brothers."

"And what are your favorites?" Alex held open the door for Sierra as they exited. She liked being treated like a princess.

"My favorite sports? I like hiking and backpacking."

"Oh, then you are going to like Switzerland very much. We must go for a hike together."

Sierra looked up at him. A wayward strand of his dark hair was just beginning to break free from the pack to form a curl. *He reminds me of Paul,* Sierra realized. Not in looks, but in manner. They both had strong personalities. And Alex looked at her the way Paul had when they first met. But Paul was older—definitely too old for Sierra. And he was far away in Scotland. Sierra was in Germany with Alex. Why was she thinking about Paul? And why would she want to compare Alex with anyone? He was unique and wonderful, and she loved that he was paying attention to her.

Mr. Pratt led them down the street four short blocks past a tidy little garden alive with columbine, sweet peas, and cherry tomatoes strung up against a low fence. He stopped at the front door of a tall, narrow, timber-framed house and said, "Please make yourselves welcome. You are my guests." He then opened the door and called out something in German.

A stout, stern-looking woman appeared before them, wearing an apron over her skirt and blouse. It seemed to Sierra that the woman was staring at them a little too obviously as Mr. Pratt spoke to her in German.

"Is that his wife?" Sierra whispered.

"No," Alex whispered back. "She died many years ago. This must be the housekeeper. He is asking her to prepare something of a meal for us. She is arguing that he didn't give her enough notice. He is going to see what there is to eat."

Sierra suppressed a giggle. It was fun having a personal interpreter. It was even more fun having him whisper in her ear.

Mr. Pratt directed them into the living room, saying he would join them in a moment. The four of them sat down. Alex, Sierra, and Christy perched on the sofa while Marti selected the winged-back chair. The living room was small but tidy. A picture of a canal and an elaborately carved bridge hung on the wall above the mantle in an intricate gold frame.

Sierra was gazing at the picture when Alex leaned over and said, "The Bridge of Sighs. In Venice, of course. Have you been there?"

"No."

"I have," Marti spoke up. "My husband, Robert, and I were there many years ago. It is a lovely city, isn't it, Alex? Overpriced accommodations, of course, but the food is good, don't you think?"

No one said anything. It seemed they were all too startled by this sudden change in Marti's treatment of Alex.

"My favorite, of course, is Paris," Marti plunged on. "No other European city compares. The food, the shopping, the museums . . . "

"Then you would like Moscow very much," Alex said.

"It is a masterpiece of a city. When it comes to museums, nothing compares with the Hermitage in St. Petersburg. You must come for a visit."

It seemed to Sierra that Marti bristled slightly. There was no mistaking her body language. The thought of visiting any part of the former Soviet Union did not appeal to her one bit.

Fortunately, Mr. Pratt arrived with a plate of cookies in his hand. His cheeks were flushed. It appeared he was more in command at his school than he was in his own home. "Please forgive me for leaving you like this. Frau Weber will be right in with the coffee. You do all drink coffee, don't you?"

Sierra nodded with the rest of them. The truth was, she rarely drank coffee. Her idea of a good hot beverage was herbal tea, especially the fruit herbal teas. Apparently, everyone in Germany liked coffee. Her dad would definitely fit in here.

Dark, strong coffee served in small china cups arrived on a tray carried by the disgruntled Frau Weber. She let the tray down with a clang on the small coffee table and turned with a huff.

"So," Mr. Pratt said, regaining his composure, "please help yourselves, and Alex do tell me how your family is doing."

Sierra enjoyed sitting back and listening to Alex talk. She held her cup of coffee carefully in her lap and took one tiny sip. Even with all the milk and sugar she had added, it was still too strong for her to stomach.

The warm August afternoon sun pouring through the open window soon made the living room feel small as Sierra sat wedged between Christy and Alex. She liked hearing about Alex's family, but she would have given anything for a glass of ice water and a seat by the window.

Alex spoke fondly of his mother and father to Mr. Pratt. Whenever he didn't know a word in English, he slipped in a German one, and Mr. Pratt would repeat the word in English for Marti, Christy, and Sierra's benefit.

Marti had recovered her charming self and even laughed at one of Alex's stories about his six-year-old sister. Sierra gave Christy a poke, and Christy poked her back. Marti's opinion of Alex had been transformed— and that could only mean good things for Sierra.

Chapter Six

*L*ATER THAT NIGHT, BACK AT THE HOTEL, Marti put Sierra's romantic hopes in check.

"Don't think for one minute," Marti said, "that I approve of you nurturing a romance with this Russian, Sierra. What would your parents think?"

Sierra knew what her parents would think. She was sure they would think she was old enough and mature enough to manage her own relationships. They always liked her friends. All of them. They would like Alex, too.

Before Sierra could defend herself to Marti, Christy stepped out of the bathroom. She was wearing her pajamas and had a toothbrush in her hand. "You saw for yourself what a great guy he is, Aunt Marti. He drove us back from the school, took us to dinner, and even paid for it himself. The guy is a gem! What's wrong with Sierra developing a new friendship? I'm all for it," she said.

"Go brush your teeth, Christina. This is between Sierra and me," Marti snapped back.

Christy stepped forward and stood next to where Sierra was seated on the bed. Marti was standing in front of Sierra, which meant Christy formed a sort of human buffer between them.

"Actually, this is between all three of us," Christy said firmly. "Sierra is my friend. She's my guest on this trip. I'm enjoying Alex's company as much as she is. And when he picks us up and takes us to the orphanage tomorrow, this will be between the four of us."

Christy's toothbrush appeared to be shaking slightly in her hand. Sierra wondered if Christy stood up to her aunt like this very often, or if she was merely appearing brave and confident.

"If it's all right with you, Aunt Marti," Christy continued, "I'd like it if the three of us could come to a mutual agreement about Alexander now, so that there won't be any awkward situations tomorrow. He's a wonderful Christian guy. He enjoys being with us and doesn't seem to mind being our tour guide. I'd like it if you would approve of Sierra's and my friendship with Alex. Please trust us, and please be nice to him."

"I've been extremely nice," Marti said defensively.

"After you found out that Mr. Pratt approved of him," Sierra said, sliding her comment in carefully. The minute she said it, Sierra knew that she should have kept quiet and let Christy calm Marti.

Marti snapped back at Sierra, "You've missed the point entirely. You met him on the train, for goodness' sake. How did you know it would be safe to spend time with him?"

Sierra paused a moment before stating calmly,

"Because he's a Christian."

Marti threw up her hands and turned her face to the ceiling. "Why can't I make you two innocent young dreamers understand what men are really like? It doesn't matter what they say. They can't be trusted. The sooner you grow up and realize that, the better off we'll all be." She shook her head and pursed her lips together. It seemed she had something more to say but was trying hard to hold it in. "You just don't know," she finally sputtered. "You two girls simply don't understand."

With that, she turned and went into her room, firmly closing the door. Sierra and Christy gave each other long, silent looks.

"What do you think she's trying to tell us?" Sierra asked. "Maybe she was burned by some guy when she was our age, and now she thinks it's her role in life to protect you and your friends from the same mistakes she made."

"Wow." Christy plopped down on the bed and stared at the closed door between the rooms. She was silent a moment. Then she said, "You could be right. I never thought of that."

"Your uncle seems so great," Sierra said. "I can't imagine him ever hurting her. Must have been some guy before Bob. Maybe some gorgeous football player broke her heart in high school."

"You have quite an imagination," Christy said.

"It could have happened. Has she ever told you anything?"

Tucking her legs under her, Christy said, "For a long time

I thought Marti was hiding something from me, and then I found out that she'd had a baby right before I was born."

"You're kidding," Sierra said, getting comfortable on the fluffy, white coverlet. "What happened?"

"The baby was premature and had brain damage or something. She died the day before I was born."

"How awful," Sierra said softly.

"I know. That's why my aunt treats me the way she does. My mom told me years ago that everything Marti would have done for her own daughter she tries to do for me."

"Has Marti ever talked to you about any of this?" Sierra asked.

"Never. My mom says Marti doesn't talk about it to anyone. Mom told me something about Bob and Marti not being able to have any more children, but I don't remember what she said. We've only talked about it once." Christy tilted her head and pulled her silky hair over her shoulder. "I never thought of what you said tonight. What if she did have her heart broken by a guy when she was young and then lost her only baby? Something like that would explain why she's so resistant to God."

"Exactly," Sierra said. "I think it would be pretty hard to trust a God who lets horrible things like that happen in your life."

Christy nodded thoughtfully. "But how much of what happens in our lives is because God lets horrible things happen, and how much of it is due to our reaping the consequences of our actions?"

"Is that what you think happened with your aunt?" Sierra asked, surprised at Christy's comment.

"Well, we've all blown it," Christy said. Her clear blue-green eyes carried a soft glow of understanding. "Even after we surrender our lives to the Lord, we still have that tendency to go our own way. And if Marti had a really wild past, a lot of her hurt and anger today probably comes from the consequences of her choices—not random acts of God."

Sierra propped her pillow against the headboard and leaned back. "I'd sure be curious to know," she said.

"Don't get your hopes up," Christy warned as she stood up, her toothbrush still in hand. "My aunt doesn't open up to anyone. Ever."

As Christy brushed her teeth, Sierra stared at the textured plaster on the ceiling. It was hard not to take Christy's warning as a personal challenge. There were ways of getting a person to open up. Badgering them sometimes worked. And if Sierra had the opportunity, she could try her relentless debating skills on Marti. No one should spend her life acting so guarded. Marti needed to unwind.

A self-righteous thought entered Sierra's mind: What if the reason she had come on this trip was to crack open Marti and make her break down some of her walls? What if Sierra was supposed to help Marti experience God's love? Sierra liked the thought that God might have chosen her for such an important task.

"You know what?" Christy said, returning from the bathroom and slipping into her bed. "I kind of like the school."

Sierra left all her Joan of Arc feelings to float on the plastered ceiling and came down to earth to join Christy. After all, the obvious reason they had come on this trip was so Christy could check out the school. The least Sierra could do was support her friend in this gigantic decision.

"Tell me your impressions of the place while I get ready for bed," Sierra said. She rummaged in her bag for her nightshirt and toothbrush.

Christy ran through a list of all the logical pluses of the school. She gave all the reasons she should go there as Sierra washed her face and brushed her teeth.

"Obviously, you think it's a great school," Sierra commented. "So why do I hear you hesitating about it?" She crawled into bed and fluffed up her pillow. "Man, this is a comfortable bed!"

"I know. Like snuggling into a cloud," Christy agreed. "Anyway, I'm just not sure because . . . "

"Don't tell me," Sierra said. "It's Todd."

"Of course."

"How does he feel about your coming here? Last week he said it was totally up to you. Did he ever give you his true opinion?"

"That is his true opinion," Christy said, resting her head on her arm. "The night before we left, Todd told me that if we're meant to be together—which I took to mean if we're supposed to get married—then this year away at school won't change things between us. He says it will only make us appreciate each other more—the way we fell more in love when he went to Spain."

"I think you two appreciate each other plenty. Why don't you just go ahead and get married? You know you're right for each other. At least, that's what everyone else thinks. Don't you two feel the same way?"

Christy's face took on a contemplative, glowing look. To Sierra, it was the look of a woman in love. "You see, Todd has always been slow," Christy explained. "Or maybe I should say 'cautious.' His parents are divorced, and he wants to be careful about his commitments and about making sure he means to keep all his promises. We've never really talked about marriage. I thought maybe we would after Doug and Tracy's wedding."

"I wish I had a picture of you and Todd when you walked out of the church arm-in-arm after the wedding ceremony," Sierra said. "You both had that Romeo-and-Juliet look down pretty well. I think Todd's hopelessly in love with you, but he isn't ready to admit it yet."

Christy smiled. "I know. And I love him. I know that. But I don't know if either of us is ready for marriage yet. Having me go away for a year might be the best thing for us. And like you said last week, we could start to write letters, which would be a whole new way to communicate for us."

"A very romantic way, too," Sierra said. "I've always dreamed of what it would be like to carry on a passionate correspondence with a guy I was crazy about."

"With Alexander, maybe?"

Christy's comment surprised Sierra. Actually, Sierra had been thinking of a correspondence with Paul. Ever since his brother, Jeremy, told Sierra a few days ago that he thought Sierra should write to Paul in Scotland, Sierra had let the idea build in her mind. Her reaction to Paul's brother had been, "If he wants to correspond, then let him write me first." She knew Paul would get the message exactly as she stated it. And somehow she also knew that Paul was just like her, and he wouldn't let go of a challenge.

"Yeah," Sierra finally said, "with Alexander."

"Wait a minute," Christy said. "You didn't sound too excited there. You weren't thinking of Alexander, were you?"

"No. Isn't that weird? After all that happened today, you would think Alex would be the only guy on my mind. I was thinking of Paul." Sierra had told Christy all about Paul, but she had never admitted to Christy or anyone else how stuck she was on him.

A slow grin spread across Christy's lips. "I didn't realize," Christy stated with an air of satisfaction.

"Realize what?"

"Paul is your Philippians 1:7 guy, isn't he?"

"My what?"

"Your Philippians 1:7 guy. Todd sent that verse to me once on a coconut from Hawaii. The verse says, 'I have you in my heart.'"

Christy sat halfway up and leaned toward Sierra. Then, as if Christy were revealing a great secret, she whispered, "Sierra, you hold Paul in your heart, don't you?"

Chapter Seven

WHEN SIERRA AWOKE THE NEXT MORNING, she felt as though she hadn't slept at all. Her dreams kept waking her through the night—and her dreams had been about Alex. When Sierra woke to the alarm, she only wanted to go back to sleep.

"Want me to shower first?" Christy mumbled.

"Be my guest. Take as much time as you want. Don't bother to wake me when you get out." Sierra turned on her side and pulled the comforter over her face to block out the brightness of the sun breaking through the window.

"Sierra," Christy said, plopping on Sierra's bed and gently shaking her shoulder, "wake up. We're in Switzerland! Alex is going to be waiting for us."

"I thought you were going to take a shower," Sierra said.

"I did. You fell back asleep. Come on. We need to get going. My aunt wants us to have breakfast downstairs with her in 15 minutes."

"All right, all right. I'm coming." Sierra sat up and tried to open her eyes. "Do I look as wiped out as I feel?"

"You'll feel better after a shower, that's for sure," Christy said. "You'll see. It's a great shower. Lots of warm water. This is going to be a wonderful day!" Christy rose from the bed and began to sort through her stack of clean clothes as she hummed a little tune.

"I can't stand perky people in the morning," Sierra blurted out as she stumbled to the shower. "You'll remember that, Christina, if you know what's good for you."

"A shower will be good for *you*," Christy called out after her.

Sierra never would have believed it, but Christy was right. Sierra emerged from the shower, feeling much more coherent than she had been 10 minutes earlier. She wrapped herself in a towel, stepped into their bedroom, and saw Christy sitting at the small corner desk, talking on the phone. She was wearing a short summer dress, and her hair was twisted on top of her head in a smooth roll, styled like many Swiss teenagers were doing. It was an elegant look, and it made Christy look five years older.

Christy looked up and smiled, still holding the phone to her ear. "So far I do. We're going to the orphanage this morning. . . . Okay, I will. You, too. . . . Okay. . . . Yeah, I promise I'll call you tomorrow at this time. . . . I miss you, too. Bye." She lowered the receiver and gazed at the silent, black phone.

"Todd?" Sierra guessed.

Christy nodded. "He called me. I was going to ask

Marti if I could call him in a few days, but he called me. He said he missed me and was praying for me. And he said to tell you hi, too. I told him about Alex."

"You did? What did he say?"

"He said he hopes you go for it."

"Go for what?" Sierra laughed, pulling on her shorts.

"You know, the relationship. The adventure. The chance to grow by giving a little part of yourself to someone special."

Sierra pulled her wrinkled T-shirt over her head and wrapped the bath towel around her wet hair. One uncooperative blond curl dangled down the right side of her face. "What are you telling me? Todd calls you all the way from California, and you spend his money discussing my love life—or rather, lack thereof?"

"Something like that," Christy said. "Remember how you told me what your dad said when he gave you your purity ring?"

Sierra glanced down at the simple gold band on her right hand. "What? That he was proud of me for setting such high standards or something?"

"No, remember after you left the restaurant? You told me your dad said to have fun while you were a teenager. Well, I agree with him. Take every relationship God brings your way, and enjoy what that person has to offer and what you can offer him. It's not all serious soul-searching when it comes to guys, you know."

Sierra put her hand on her hip. "You and Todd discussed all this while I was in the shower? Maybe we should have had a conference call so I could have received this advice right from the Big Kahuna's mouth."

"No," Christy said with a laugh, "we didn't discuss all this. I've just been thinking about it ever since you told me what your dad said, and I think he's right. You have to take a chance and open your heart to people, Sierra."

"You don't think I do?"

Before Christy could answer, Marti called through their closed door, "Are you two ready?"

"Almost," Christy called back.

Marti opened the door. She looked fully rested and ready to go in her straight denim skirt and freshly pressed white blouse. Her eyebrows crashed together when she saw Sierra with a towel wrapped like a turban around her head.

"You're not ready," she stated.

"We almost are," Christy said. "Can we meet you downstairs in a few minutes?"

"Do hurry," Marti said with a drawn-out sigh. "I'll be waiting for you in the dining room."

As the day proceeded, Marti's patience was tried half a dozen more times. It seemed she spent most of the day waiting for Sierra and Christy. First, they were late for breakfast, and then when Alex arrived, the girls had to run up to their room to pick up their backpacks.

When they met Alex and Marti at the car, Marti was planted in the front passenger seat. Alex opened the back door for Sierra.

As she climbed inside, Alex leaned toward her and said

softly, "It is wonderful to see you again, See-hair-a."

Before she could respond, he gently brushed the back of his hand across her cheek. It was the most tender, affectionate gesture she had ever experienced, and it almost made her heart stop.

"It's good to see you, too," she said, her voice suddenly turning hoarse.

When they arrived at the orphanage, Alex offered Sierra his hand as she exited the backseat. He held it only a moment before opening Marti's door and offering her a hand as well.

She politely refused and walked ahead of them into the orphanage, stating over her shoulder, "We're 10 minutes late, you know. They might not let us in."

The staff woman who greeted them assured Marti their late arrival was no problem, and they could take the tour now. Marti made it only to the first hallway on the first floor before she excused herself, saying she felt jet-lagged; but they should go ahead and take their time. She would wait outside for them on the long bench in front of the building.

Sierra and Christy exchanged glances. Sierra assumed it was difficult for Marti to be around so many children since she had lost her only child. Or maybe all the references to Christianity their hostess used as she explained the mission and philosophy of the orphanage had disturbed Marti.

Sierra felt drawn in and intrigued by the orphanage. She knew Christy was feeling the same way. Alex's presence added a deeper level of understanding as he quietly provided insights during their tour. Many children were from Africa, but most were from Bosnia. Some were Serbs, some were Croatians. Now everything Sierra had heard on the news about Bosnia had a face. These children were no longer faraway victims. The suffering was right here before her, and it was very real.

The sheer number of children in the orphanage disturbed Sierra. Their hostess said currently more than 300 orphans lived there, but only 3 percent of those would ever be adopted. There were so many children! Sierra's heart ached for them.

The building was once a factory and was large enough to hold even more kids. The guide said it had housed more than 425 orphans a few years earlier. The structure was restored with fresh whitewash on the walls and newer fixtures in the bathrooms. It was actually better-looking and cleaner on the inside than it was on the outside. The efficient Swiss staff all wore tidy uniforms and appeared to run a tight ship.

Even though the children were clean, well fed, and looked as if they were being cared for, Sierra could tell something was missing. Their eyes all had the same sad look. They longed for a mother and father's love. Sierra knew their empty little faces would haunt her for the rest of her life.

After they had finished their hour and a half tour of the facilities, Christy, Sierra, and Alex joined Marti out front. She looked as if she were nearly at the end of her patience rope.

Alex offered to take them to lunch, and Marti accepted for them, briskly stating that this time she would pay.

"I know just the place we can go," Alex said, opening the car door for Marti. "This will be a real treat."

Then, opening Sierra's door, Alex gave Sierra's shoulder a gentle squeeze. She wondered if he was feeling the same way she was. They had looked into the face of terrible injustice. Any personal, earthly luxury seemed selfish. Lunch did not appeal to her.

Alex pulled out into the moving traffic. All around them, the summer day glowed. Sierra opened her window. It only went down halfway, but it was enough for the scents and sounds of Basel to come rushing into the car. She noticed a sign above a large old building that said in English: "The Salvation Army." It looked like a second-hand shop as well as a soup kitchen, similar to the Highland House in Portland, where she volunteered one day a week. Suddenly, the world seemed rather small. The poor and needy, orphans and sick people, were everywhere. It was overwhelming to think of how much help humanity needed.

"Is that the train station where we came in?" Christy asked, interrupting Sierra's thoughts.

"Yes. That one is the Badisher Bahnhof," Alex said, pointing to the station as they passed. Two cement lion statues guarded the entrance. Sierra hadn't noticed them before. Lions always made her think of Aslan from the

Narnia tales, and Aslan made her think of Christ.

Does all this pain in the world break your heart, too, Lord? It must.

Sierra thought about the conversation she'd had with Christy the night before. Christy had said that some of life's problems are "acts of God"—circumstances we may never understand—while other problems are the direct result or consequence of our sins. But Sierra knew that those 300 children hadn't done anything to deserve being orphaned.

As Alex drove across the Rhine River, Sierra gazed into the slow-moving waters and blinked back tears. This morning, those children had become her neighbors and were no longer distant images on TV. Pain in life was real.

Chapter Eight

"**M**cDonald's!" Marti blurted out in disbelief. "You've brought us to a McDonald's?"

"Yes," Alex said proudly, looking for a parking place along the crowded street. "This is a very popular place for the university students. I thought Christy would like to see it."

"Well, we've seen it," Marti remarked. "Remember where this is, Christy. Now let's go find a nice, quiet café."

"You do not wish to eat here?" Alex sounded baffled. "You can always find a small restaurant, but McDonald's are not so many."

"They are everywhere in America," Marti said. "And if I don't eat at McDonald's in America, I'm certainly not going to eat at one in Switzerland."

"We will drive on, then," Alex said.

Sierra appreciated his flexibility, although she liked Alex's idea. She wanted to go inside the McDonald's to compare it with the ones at home.

They found a small, outdoor café with several open

tables. Alex parked the car, and they sat under a green-and-white umbrella at a round table. The menu was limited. Marti ordered a salad and was sorely disappointed. At Alex's suggestion, Christy and Sierra ordered the Nurnbergers. What they got was actually a type of small hot dog or sausage. Alex also suggested they order Schwip Schwap to drink. It came to them in glasses, lukewarm, with no ice.

"I forgot about this part of European dining," Christy said as she tried her drink. "They don't put ice in the drinks."

"Do you like the Schwip Schwap?" Alex asked. "It was always my favorite when I was young."

To Sierra, it seemed terribly sweet. A sort of "suicide" combination of orange, lemon, and cola mixed together. It tasted flat without the ice. "It's different from what we drink at home," she said. She was still unsettled by her experience at the orphanage—her lunch was not appealing.

"I've been thinking about why the orphanage asks the students to make a one-year commitment to the program," Christy said. "Can you imagine how hard it is on those children to always have people they love leave them? That's the only thing that scares me about coming here."

"The children?" Marti asked.

"Being with them for so long and then having to leave," Christy explained.

"Gracious, Christina, you haven't even decided if you're going to attend the school, and already you're turning melancholy over leaving. You don't know how it will be until you come. You might be glad to leave after one year. The purpose is your education, not to save the world."

"Have you decided to come?" Alex asked.

His seat was the only one in the direct sunshine. He had put on a pair of slim sunglasses and was leaning back in his chair. Sierra thought he looked very different from the guys she hung out with at her Christian high school in Portland. Even though he was wearing a T-shirt and jeans, Alex looked like someone who had already lived a lifetime.

"I don't know for sure," Christy said. "Part of me is ready to sign up and start school here right now. Another part wants to go home and pretend this corner of the world is only something I imagined."

"It's real," Alex said. "All of it. But it's as real as your life in California. I am of the belief that it does not matter where one lives or what one does so long as everything revolves around God. Time is short."

Sierra shot a quick glance at Marti to see how Alex's words affected her. She hid her reaction well.

"You know," Christy said, leaning forward and not looking at Marti at all, "sometimes I think about that, too. I keep hearing more and more about the end-times and how Christ is coming back, and it makes me wonder what I should be doing. I mean, if we are living in the end-times, then shouldn't I be more concerned about witnessing to people rather than pursuing my education?"

Sierra had never thought of that.

"We should get going," Marti said.

Alex gave a slight nod; then, removing his sunglasses, he leaned in and looked intently at Christy. "Whatever God shows you to do, the reason should be always a . . . what was that word?" He reached into his back pocket and pulled out a small New Testament. Flipping through the pages, he found what he was looking for. "Here it is. This is Peter One in the fourth chapter."

"Do you mean First Peter?" Sierra asked.

"Yes, First Peter." Alex's strong face clouded over. "I know this in Russian and German. I do not know this word in English. It means 'very strong, coming out of the heart.'"

"Wait," Sierra said. "I have a Bible here in my backpack. What's the verse?" She pulled out her Bible and looked to see where Alex was pointing in his German New Testament. "Okay, here it is. First Peter 4:7–8: 'But the end of all things is at hand; therefore be serious and watchful in your prayers. And above all things have fervent love for one another.'"

"Yes!" Alex exclaimed. "That is the word: *fervent.* This is a strong, steady love. This is what you must consider, Christy. Whatever you do, do it with a fervent love."

"There's some more here," Sierra said, reading on in the chapter. " '. . . for "love covers over a multitude of sins." Be hospitable to one another without grumbling. As each one has received a gift, minister it to one another, as good stewards of the manifold grace of God.' "

"We simply must get back to the hotel," Marti said abruptly.

The three of them turned to look at her.

"Why?" Sierra asked.

"If you must know, I have a terrible headache. I tried to keep going so as not to spoil the day for everyone else, but now I must lie down."

"We will then go," Alex said, rising from the table and putting his Bible back in his pocket. He helped to pull out Marti's chair and offered her his arm.

"I'm not an invalid," she snapped. "I can get myself to the car."

As they drove back to the hotel, Sierra thought about the verses they had read. *"Love each other fervently." Do I know what that means? I love people, but is my love strong and steady?*

When they were about a block from the hotel, Alex calmly asked Marti, "Would it be all right with you if I show Christy and See-hair-a some of the other sights of Basel?"

"I don't think that's such a good idea," Marti said. "I think this is where we say good-bye. You've been quite gracious, and I do thank you."

Alex stopped in front of the hotel, and a uniformed attendant opened the car door for Marti and offered her a white-gloved hand to help her out. Alex opened the door for Christy and Sierra. He took hold of Sierra's elbow and gave it a little squeeze.

Sierra looked up into Alexander's dark eyes and

knew that if he asked her right now to sneak out tonight, she would do it.

"I'm sure Aunt Marti will change her mind once she feels a little better," Christy said to Alex in a low voice. "Thanks for everything. Really. I appreciate it more than I can say. Not only the ride, but also your advice and encouragement."

"Girls," Marti called over her shoulder, "come now. Good-bye, Alex. And thank you."

Alex leaned over and touched his cheek against Sierra's. It happened so fast, she felt the blood rush to her face.

"I will call," he whispered.

Sierra nodded.

He got back into the car and drove away. Sierra looked over her shoulder and watched him leave.

She didn't speak again until the door was securely closed between their room and Marti's. "Did you see that?" she asked Christy.

"Did he kiss you?"

"No. He touched my cheek with his cheek. Just barely. Is that a local custom or something?"

"I don't know, but it looked pretty romantic." Christy smiled and kicked off her shoes. "I hope he calls you."

"Do you think it would be okay if we sneaked out to see him?"

"Why do you ask that?"

Sierra walked across the room and looked out the window. "Because you and I know he's wonderful and being with him is wonderful, not to mention spiritually uplifting. But your aunt doesn't understand that because she's not a Christian."

"I don't think that makes it okay to go against her wishes," Christy said.

Sierra let out a sigh. "There has to be some way to justify it. I'd rather be sight-seeing with Alex than confined to the hotel. Wouldn't you?"

"Yes," Christy said. She took the bobby pins from her hair and shook it so it fell freely over her shoulders. "But right now, I think we should take a nap."

"I hate to admit this, but I could fall asleep in a second," Sierra agreed, going over to her bed and running her hand over the comforter before flopping down. "But won't we have a hard time sleeping tonight?"

"I won't," Christy said, her eyes closed. She had stretched out and looked blissful.

"Wake me when Alex calls." Sierra rolled over onto her side and adjusted the pillow under her head.

"No way," Christy murmured. "If the phone rings, you answer it. He'll be calling for you, anyway."

"Okay," Sierra agreed. It was her last word before floating off to dreamland.

Chapter Nine

HE EARLY EVENING SHADOWS WERE STRETCHED across the wall of their hotel room when Sierra forced open her eyes. "Christy?" she mumbled. Sierra turned to see her friend snoozing in the same position she was in when she fell asleep.

Quietly rising, Sierra tiptoed over to the window. She liked the view from here. Across the road stood a large building that had the name *Rathaus* carved into its wall. She knew that meant it was the community or municipal building. There had been one in Germany, too, where the Schwarzwald Volkschule was located, and Alex had explained that every small town had one.

This one in Basel was painted a deep reddish color, the shade of bricks. Along one side was a mural of larger-than-life townspeople during the Middle Ages. Around the edges was a bright gold leafing. The area surrounding the Rathaus was cobblestone, and a row of shops in tall, building-block style structures lined the street. They had to be old, hundreds of years old. But the buildings were kept up nicely with flower boxes in all the second-story

windows. The boxes spilled their apple-red ge
over the sides. Sierra found the view soothing.

Behind the shops and the Rathaus, the evening sky
busily rolled up its turquoise carpet. Sierra imagined that
somewhere up there, God was preparing to unfurl night's
inky black rug, the black rug that was sprinkled with tiny
holes. At least that's what her Granna Mae had always told
Sierra when she was little. Granna Mae had said God
decided not to repair those ancient pinpoints in the
nighttime carpet because all those holes let the brilliance
of heaven peep through.

I'm in Switzerland, she reminded herself. *This city must
be beautiful at night. What if Alex and I went out tonight
and strolled these ancient streets? Now* that *would be
romantic.*

The phone rang. Sierra jumped. Actually, the noise it
made was a warbling, electrical sound rather than a ring.
She grabbed the receiver and said, "Hello, Alex?"

"Oh, I must have the wrong room," a familiar voice on
the other end said. "I'm sorry."

"No, wait!" Sierra said before the male voice was cut
off. "Dad?"

"Sierra?"

"Yes, it's me. Hi."

"Hi. How are you doing?" her dad asked.

"Fine. We're all doing great. Tired, but I was expecting
that. How are you guys? Is everything okay?"

"Yes. Terrific. We were just missing you, and I wanted
to see how everything was going."

Sierra gave her dad a quick rundown on the orphanage and the school.

"Good," he said. "And who is Alex?"

Sierra smiled, pausing before she spoke. Her dad never missed a beat. He knew all six of his kids so well. He had earned their respect, and the kids welcomed his involvement in their lives.

She told her dad about meeting Alex on the train, how he had turned out to be Mr. Pratt's close friend, and how he had been showing them the sights.

"Sounds like a great guy," Mr. Jensen said, "but I'm going to give you one fatherly command here. Are you ready?"

"Yes."

"Make sure Christy is always with you when you see him these next few days."

"Why?"

"A precaution, that's all."

"Dad, you would really like him. He's a super-strong Christian."

"I don't doubt it," her dad said. "And I hope you two have some really wonderful, memorable times together. Use the buddy system, though. Make sure Christy is always with you, okay?"

"Don't you trust me?"

"We trust you completely."

"Then what's the big deal?" Sierra asked incredulously.

"Oh, a couple thousand miles," he replied. "Your spending time with a guy in Switzerland isn't quite the same as having Randy over here for dinner."

"Randy's just a buddy."

"Okay, then Drake."

"I only went out with him once," Sierra said.

"Sierra."

She could tell by the firmness in her father's voice that it was time to stop the banter. Dad meant business.

"If, or should I say when, you see Alex again, you must be with Christy or Marti the whole time. Those are the orders from headquarters," he said.

"Got it." Sierra tried to sound lighthearted. The last thing she wanted to do was upset her dad or have him think she was going against his rules. He had been right too many times for her to second-guess his reasoning. "Say hi to Mom and everyone for me."

"Will do. You have a great time, now, okay?"

"I will. Thanks for calling. I love you guys."

"We love you, too. Bye, honey."

The click on the other end signaled the phone call was over, but the warmth of her dad's voice remained. Sierra had awesome parents, and she knew it.

"Was that Alex?" Christy asked, shaking off her jet lag as she sat up and stretched.

"No, it was my dad. Can you believe that? Here I'm thinking how wonderful it would be to sneak out to see Alex, and my dad calls and asks me to promise I'll only spend time with Alex if we're with you or Marti."

"Sounds like something my dad would say," Christy observed.

"And would you do what he said?"

"Probably." Christy stretched again and yawned. "I sneaked out once on a trip with my aunt and uncle to Palm Springs."

"You?" Sierra sounded shocked.

"Yes, some of my friends and me. It was so dumb. Now when I think about it, I can't believe I let them talk me into it."

"Was it to see a guy?"

"No," Christy said, getting up and going over to the window to look out at the view. "We sneaked out to go to a store. It turned into a huge mess. We ended up at the police station, and everyone was mad at me for a long time. Definitely not worth the risk."

Sierra believed Christy when she said it was a bad idea. Sierra knew that her dad made the chaperone rule only because he loved her. Still, she couldn't deny that if Alex called and wanted to see her tonight, she would still be tempted to go.

But Alex didn't call. Marti woke up shortly after Christy did and briskly proclaimed her headache had gone away. Marti insisted the three of them go downstairs to the hotel restaurant for dinner even though it was after eight o'clock.

They were all hungrier than they thought, and the Wiener schnitzel and potatoes tasted wonderful. With their spirits renewed, they decided to take a stroll and window-shop in what their waiter had called the *alt stadt*, or old town, of Basel.

A cool breeze skittered off the Rhine River and kept them company as the three women walked and talked. They got along better than they had at any other time on their trip.

Sierra was hopeful that, if Marti stayed in this good mood, she might agree to let Sierra spend more time with Alex. Maybe they could go hiking as he had suggested. Or at least for a picnic or bike ride.

Ever since Sierra had arrived in Europe, Alex had been a part of everything she had done. It would be miserable to try to see the sights without him.

"Would you like to visit the school again tomorrow, Christy?" Marti asked as they looked in one of the shop windows. "Are there any unanswered questions you would like to discuss with Mr. Pratt?"

"No, I think I have a pretty good idea of what it's all about. I just need to decide if I'm going to attend or not before we leave."

"Yes, you do," Marti agreed.

"I'd like to do some more sight-seeing," Christy said. Then she added smoothly, "A hike with Alex would be especially fun."

To Sierra's surprise, Marti didn't immediately rebuff Christy. They were nearly back at the hotel.

"Marti, I don't know if this helps you decide," Sierra said, "but when my dad called tonight, I told him about Alex. Dad said he hoped we would spend more time together, have fun, and make some memories."

"Your father said that?" Marti asked. "You're not making this up, are you?"

"No, that's what he said. He also said that whatever I did with Alex had to be with Christy or with you."

"That's what he told you?"

"Yes," Sierra said firmly. She wasn't used to having her word questioned.

"Then I must say I applaud you for telling me. Honesty is always the best policy."

"Yes, I guess it is," Sierra said, more to herself than to Marti.

Marti stopped walking and turned to face Sierra and Christy with one of the nicest expressions she had worn on the trip. It was obvious she was feeling better. "I must say I admire the two of you for the way you abide by your parents' directions. You are both quite different from how I was at your age."

"I hear you were pretty wild," Sierra said, seizing her opportunity to delve in. Christy pinched her. "I mean, I can just imagine you must have been rowdy if you were so different from us," Sierra said quickly, trying to cover her blunder. "Christy and I are actually pretty boring people when it comes down to it."

"Speak for yourself," Christy teased.

Marti resumed walking in step with Christy and Sierra. A moment later, she asked, "Christy, what has your mother said about me?"

"Nothing."

"No, you can tell me. What has Margaret been saying?"

"All she ever said was that you two were pretty opposite, and I know my mom was super obedient and had a boring social life."

"My social life was never boring, that's for sure."

"What was it like?" Sierra said, barging into the conversation. She thought this might be the right time for her to start tearing down the walls that Marti had built.

"That's quite a bold question," Marti said. She sounded surprised but not offended.

"Did you have lots of boyfriends?" Sierra asked. "I picture you with the captain of the football team or maybe the star basketball player. You would have made a cute couple—a tall guy and you, a sweet, petite girl."

Marti laughed. "He was actually a hockey player. And he wasn't all that tall. Just muscular and, oh, so aggressive! I believed he could stop the world from rotating if I only asked. Nelson was definitely a self-made guy. What Nelson wanted, Nelson got."

"That was his first name?" Sierra asked. "Nelson?"

Marti suddenly looked surprised, as if she hadn't realized what she had said. "You girls don't need to hear this. Forget I brought it up. That was all very long ago. What we should be doing is discussing our plans for tomorrow. Why don't we plan on breakfast at eight? We'll meet downstairs as we did this morning, only please try to be on time tomorrow. We can take it from there. I think some shopping is in order, don't you?"

Sierra wasn't ready to think about shopping. She had uncovered a corner of Marti's armor, and the name tattooed there was "Nelson."

Chapter Ten

"**N**ELSON," SIERRA REPEATED TO CHRISTY once they were back in their room. "Have you ever met anyone named Nelson?"

"No."

"I wonder what happened with him. She almost told us—did you notice that?" Sierra asked.

Christy nodded. "She was in a good mood, too. That was nice."

"Let's hope her good mood sticks around for a while."

The next morning Marti was still in a good mood when they met downstairs for breakfast. Sierra might have tried to make another crack in Marti's armor except, this time, Sierra was the one in a foul mood.

She hadn't slept well. The nap had thrown her off, and so she wasn't able to fall asleep right away like Christy had. Instead, Sierra lay in the quiet room thinking and praying, half awake and half asleep for hours.

It didn't help that Alex hadn't called. *Why do guys do that?* Sierra fumed to herself. *They say they'll call, they act sweet and even touch your cheek like they mean to keep their*

promise, and then you never hear from them. Here I was
thinking of what it would be like to sneak out, and then he
doesn't even call!

The more she thought about her previous urge to
sneak out, the worse she felt. She wouldn't even dream of
doing something like that at home. Why had she allowed
herself to think it would be okay here? All she could
come up with was, at home, she respected her parents and
their authority over her. She didn't feel exactly the same
about Marti.

"We can start with shops down the street where
we went for our walk last night," Marti suggested after
breakfast. "I especially wanted to go back and buy that
scarf I saw about two blocks down. Was there anything in
particular you girls saw that you wanted?"

"Nope," Christy said. She had awakened in a sunny
mood. When Sierra emerged from the shower, Christy
had been seated at the desk, reading her Bible, writing in
her journal, and humming. Sierra threw a pillow at her,
but that didn't stop her happy little tune.

They entered the first shop, and Sierra watched Marti
turn into a different person. She greeted the friendly sales
clerks and began to make flattering comments about their
merchandise. The clerks moved in closer and responded
to her in their professional English. Marti was in control.

"Why do you think Alex didn't call?" Sierra asked
Christy.

They hung back in the front corner of the store next to
a display of greeting cards.

"He probably had a good reason."

"Yeah, like, he's a guy and all guys are alike. They come across all sweet and interested, and then someone more interesting catches their attention and suddenly, you're nothing to them."

Christy laughed softly.

"I wish you wouldn't mock me when I'm sulking." Sierra crossed her arms and gave Christy an exaggerated pout.

"It's funny," Christy said. "Not what you're feeling, but what you're saying sounds exactly like what I used to say about Todd a few years ago."

"Great. Now you're telling me that even Dream Boy Todd used to be an insensitive jerk. Is there no hope?"

"Oh, I could tell you stories! There's enough to fill a book." Christy leaned closer. "Todd has still been known to have occasional setbacks. Like with this trip. This is a big decision for me, and I think it involves Todd, too. But he keeps acting like it doesn't matter. Whatever I want to do will be fine with him. Makes me so mad when I think about it."

"I'm sure he's only trying to be nice and give you freedom to make your own decision."

"Are you defending him?" Christy said, now crossing her arms as well.

"Somebody should," Sierra remarked.

She and Christy eyed each other.

At that moment, Sierra realized that if she looked half as silly as Christy did, both standing there in their mutual pout positions, the two of them must be a hilarious sight. She started to laugh.

"What?" Christy said.

"Guys," Sierra said with a glimmer in her eye. "Who needs 'em?"

"That's right," Christy agreed. "Who needs them? We're in Switzerland, for goodness' sake! We need to start having our own fun and forget about Todd and Alex."

"I'm with you," Sierra said. "We have the whole day ahead of us without a single guy on the schedule. What do you want to do?"

"I'm sure Marti wants to shop some more, but then she always wants to shop." Christy looked over at her aunt. "If you see anything, be sure to speak up. She'll buy it for you. I think her hobby is buying things for people."

"You mean her hobbit," Sierra said.

"Her what?"

"That's what Alex said instead of 'hobby.' "

"Alex?" Christy challenged. "I thought we were done with those undependable guys. It's just us women today."

"You're right," Sierra said, holding up her arm as if she were the Statue of Liberty. "Onward to freedom and liberty and shaking off our emotional chains."

As she spoke the last two words, her fist hit a revolving rack of note cards and tipped the rack off balance. It teetered dangerously.

"Look out!" Christy yelled to one of the customers who was heading for the door and about to be clobbered by the card rack.

Sierra's quick reflexes enabled her to catch the edge of the rack, and she jerked it back toward herself. The rack didn't hit the startled customer, but a dozen packets of note cards ejected in the sudden yank and pummeled the unsuspecting woman like snowballs. The rack, responding to Sierra's quick pull, toppled in the other direction. It landed on the greeting cards, crumpling dozens of them as it continued its crash course to the floor, where it pulled out the electric cord along the wall, causing the overhead lights and fans to turn off.

Everything suddenly went silent. Everyone in the store turned to stare at Sierra and Christy. A salesclerk marched over and plugged the lights and fan back in.

"Quick!" Sierra said under her breath. "How do you say 'Excuse me' in German?"

"Sorry," Christy blurted out. "Pardon us. *Merci. Por favor.*"

"That's not German!" Sierra hissed through her clenched smile.

"It was the best I could do," Christy said.

She helped Sierra right the toppled rack and began to scoop up the packages of note cards.

"Are you all right?" Sierra asked the still startled customer.

The woman answered in French and then in German. When Sierra understood neither, the shopper swatted her hand in the air and exited the shop.

"What happened?" Marti demanded, flying to their corner of the store.

"It was an accident," Christy said, calmly placing the note cards back in the rack. "Oh, these are cute. Did you see these with the wildflowers, Sierra?"

"Let's get some," Sierra suggested, placing the last of the note cards onto the rack.

"Couldn't you have decided they were cute without causing the entire display to fall apart?" Marti snapped. "They're ruined, so we'll have to buy all of them."

"They're not ruined," Sierra said. "They're packaged in these sturdy plastic boxes. But the cards are a different story." She turned to look behind her. At least two dozen greeting cards were mangled.

Marti marched over and began to snap up the bent cards. She even took ones that were not bent but were in the vicinity of the damaged ones.

"You two wait outside and try not to destroy anything else, will you?" Marti whooshed past them and went to pay for the cards. Sierra and Christy silently left the small store and walked over to a streetlight to wait for Marti. A basket of bright yellow marigolds and tiny blue flowers hung over their heads.

"Don't do any more liberated-woman imitations, Sierra, or you'll bring that flower basket down on your head," Christy warned with a laugh.

"Is your aunt so annoyed that she'll never want to see me again?"

"She'll be okay. Don't worry about it. It was an accident. Besides, we got a year's supply of German greeting cards out of the deal. That might not have happened if the rack hadn't come after you."

They both started to laugh.

"I want the cards," Sierra said. "I think we should send them to all our friends and let them guess what the German greeting says."

"Let's do it!" Christy agreed. "They probably say, 'Sorry to hear about your kidney stones,' or 'Congratulations on your retirement.'"

"Probably!" Sierra agreed. She shielded her eyes from the sun and looked across the street at a small wooden booth that was painted white and had green shutters. It looked like a playhouse complete with window boxes brimming with masses of orange, yellow, and blue flowers. "What is that little place? I didn't see it last night when we walked along here."

"It looks like an information booth. They probably have free maps. Should we get one?"

"Sure," Sierra said, leading the way across the cobblestone street.

An older man smoking a thin-stemmed pipe and wearing lederhosen and a green felt hat greeted them.

"*Guten tag,*" he said with a nod.

"Do you speak English?" Christy asked.

"Of course," he said.

"Is this an information booth?" she asked.

He silently raised his gray eyes to the large information sign above his head.

"We'd like a map," Sierra said, tucking her head in next to Christy's. "Do you have one that shows all the interesting places to go in Basel?"

"Yes." He handed them a brightly colored map with directions in four languages. "What would you like to see?" he asked.

"I'd like to go on a picnic in the Alps," Sierra said suddenly. "Like in *The Sound of Music.*"

"That was in Austria," Christy said.

"I know, but Austria and Switzerland share the same mountains, don't they? I think a picnic would be fun. We could take a bus, couldn't we? The taxis are so expensive."

"Yes, you can take a bus or you can take a train. Which mountain range would you like to see?"

Sierra shrugged. "Any of them. I like all mountains. Isn't the Matterhorn in Switzerland?"

"Yes, you could take a trip to Zermatt," the man said, opening a map of Switzerland all the way.

"I didn't mean an overnight trip. Just a day trip. For today. I thought we could go on a picnic today," Sierra said.

The man closed the map. "Then perhaps you would allow me to make another suggestion."

He opened a smaller map and, with a red pen, marked the bus line they should take. He pointed across the street to a yellow building where they would stand to catch the bus. When Christy and Sierra turned to see where he was pointing, they both saw Marti at the same time. She was pacing back and forth in front of the store with a frenzied look on her face.

"This is great. Thank you," Christy said, reaching for the map and hurrying across the street.

"*Danke,*" Sierra called over her shoulder. She knew
Marti would be hopping mad that they hadn't told her
where they were going. Their plan had been innocent—a
quick detour before Marti got out of the store.

There she stood, her fist punched into her waist and
her toe tapping. In her hand, she held a bag filled with
mangled German greeting cards.

Chapter Eleven

"**I'M NOT UPSET,**" Marti said. With purposeful steps, she led Christy and Sierra down the street toward the scarf shop. "You explained the situation to me, and like I said, next time just tell me where you're going. You can imagine how I felt when I stepped out of the shop, having covered the expense of your catastrophe, only to discover you were nowhere to be found. How would *you* feel? I was terrified. I'm responsible for the two of you, and if anything ever happened, why, I'd never recover from it."

"We're really sorry," Christy said, keeping step with her aunt.

"I know. I accepted your apology the first time you offered it. Now let's stay together, and everything will be fine."

Sierra thought for a moment that it might have been better if Marti had exploded and yelled at them. It was terrible to go through her drawn-out scolding and repeated instructions. They entered the scarf shop, and Sierra and Christy played the roles of interested and attentive nieces, helping Marti select three scarves.

"I believe the next stop should be a clothing store for you, Sierra. You said you would like to buy a dress or perhaps a new skirt. I want to treat you. Did you see a shop that interested you along the way, or should we keep going?"

"It's okay, really," Sierra began. Christy pressed her finger into Sierra's back. It had become Christy's signal to tell Sierra not to argue with Marti. "Actually, I saw a shop about three doors back that had some gauze skirts in the window."

"Gauze skirts?" Marti questioned. "Those hippie clothes?"

Sierra paused before nodding. "We could look there."

"If you're sure that's what you want."

Marti led the way to the shop. When they entered, the fragrance of heavy incense greeted them. Little bells chimed over the door, and exotic music played in the background. Posters with satanic emblems hung on the walls, and fake green snakes crawled out of the ceiling. Sierra immediately turned around and went back outside.

"That was not my kind of shop," she said.

"Well, I should hope not," Marti said.

"I like natural-looking clothes like the ones in their window, but that's all I like. The clothes are nice, but the other stuff they're promoting in there isn't."

"Why don't we keep going down the street," Christy suggested. "There are lots more shops."

The threesome slowed their pace a little as the sun

warmed them and more people crowded the streets. To Sierra, it felt as if they were in the States and this was an elite outdoor shopping center built to resemble an old European marketplace. Only this was the real thing. People speaking different languages brushed past them while the scent of strong black coffee wafted from the tiny sidewalk bakeries. In all the windows, the small shops displayed their finest wares behind thick glass, hoping to entice shoppers into their stores.

Marti, Sierra, and Christy lingered at a shop that sold nothing but tea. The wall behind the long mahogany counter was lined from ceiling to floor with dozens of bins of loose tea leaves. The scent of the mixtures filled the room. Each time Sierra drew in a breath of the fruit teas, black teas, and rich Ceylon and oolong leaves, she felt as if she had just tasted something delicious.

"I have to buy some," she said to Marti and Christy. "Do you guys mind waiting a minute? I'd like to get in line and buy some tea."

"Here's some money," Marti said.

"Thanks, but I have enough. I'm only going to buy a small bag."

Sierra studied the names of various teas as she made her way forward in line. Every time a customer pointed to a bin, one of the two white-aproned clerks pulled it open and ladled out the leaves with a metal scoop. The tea was weighed in kilos, Sierra noticed. She decided a half a kilo would be more than enough. Using gestures, nods, and the clerk's heavily accented English, Sierra was able to buy exactly what she wanted: jasmine spice. It smelled wonderful. She felt sophisticated and cultured. They exited the shop, leaving the exotic aromas behind as the door shut.

"That was fun," Sierra said. "Thanks for being patient."

"Not a problem," Marti said, pulling a lipstick tube from her purse and dabbing some color on her lips. "I could use a drink and maybe some lunch. How about you girls?"

"Do they have water anywhere in this country?" Sierra asked. "With all the snow on the Alps, you would think a drinking fountain would be on every corner."

"In here," Marti said, directing them into a bakery. "Bottled water is in the refrigerated case, Sierra. What would you like, Christy?"

"One of those," Christy said, pointing to a fat, flaky, blond-colored pastry in the case. A thin line of chocolate was drizzled over the delicacy.

The minute Sierra saw it, she said, "Definitely one of those for me, too."

Marti stepped forward and ordered for the girls. Sierra noticed that once again Marti's voice rose. She seemed to think the clerks could understand her only if she spoke loudly and exaggerated each word.

The trio took the white, glossy pastry bags outside. A father and son were leaving their seats on a window bench, providing an open seat for their group. Saying something in German, the man motioned for them to sit down. They nodded their thanks, and all three squeezed onto the brightly painted red bench.

"This is heaven," Sierra said, turning her face up to catch the warmth of the midday sun as she devoured her first bite of pastry. "What do they put in these? Mrs. Kraus needs this recipe so she can add these to the menu at Mama Bear's."

"It's probably marzipan," Marti commented. "Very popular in their pastries here."

"What kind did you get?" Sierra asked Marti.

"Nothing. A diet Coke is all I wanted."

"How can you be in Switzerland in a bakery like that and not get anything?" Sierra asked. This time Christy didn't try to stop her.

"Think of all the butter and sugar in those rolls!" Marti said.

"I don't have to think," Christy said. "I'm experiencing it."

"It will go right to your thighs," Marti warned.

"Here, have a bite of mine," Sierra urged.

"No, thank you."

"Come on! One little bite. It tastes incredible! When are you ever going to be able to get a pastry like this again—and especially in Switzerland?" Sierra broke off the end of her roll using the bag as a glove and offered the sweet to Marti. "Please. Try it."

"I don't know why it's such an issue for you," Marti said.

Christy leaned over and said, "Come on, Aunt Martha! You're going to walk off all those calories this afternoon anyhow. Live a little!"

Shaking her short dark hair to show she'd given in, Marti reached over and took the chunk of pastry from Sierra. The two girls waited for Marti's response.

Marti reluctantly drew the dainty morsel to her mouth and slowly took a bite. "Oh, that was good!" she said, savoring the pastry.

Sierra and Christy both giggled. "We told you! Go back in there and buy one for yourself."

"Do you think I should?" Marti's expression was like a little girl's. The transformation from dictator to uncertain child amazed Sierra.

"Definitely," Christy said. "If you don't go in there and buy one, Sierra and I are going to buy you one—and you know what happens when the two of us are let loose in these small shops."

"Say no more," Marti said, holding up a hand. "I'm on my way." She sprang from her seat. Grinning coyly over her shoulder, Marti entered the shop.

"You know," Sierra said, tearing off a piece of her pastry, "I like your aunt when she's on sugar."

Christy laughed. "She's a complex woman, isn't she?" Christy held up a piece of pastry and slowly placed it in her mouth.

"She's exhausted," Sierra said.

"I thought she said she slept well last night."

"No, I mean she's exhausted from hiding something deep inside for so long. It keeps trying to leak out, and she spends most of her time on guard, making sure she doesn't let up and allow her pain to surface."

"Whose psych book did you read?" Christy said, turning to study Sierra.

"Nobody's. It's only my humble opinion. You don't have to agree with it."

"That's the scary part. It makes sense. I might agree with you."

"All we have to do is wait for the right moment and ask the right question, and she'll let it all out," Sierra said.

"Don't count on it," Christy said.

The bell over the pastry shop door jingled, and Marti stepped out with her own glossy, white pastry bag in hand and a mischievous grin on her face.

She sat down and said in a lowered voice, "I also got us truffles. Did you see their chocolates? World class. Absolutely exquisite. Here's one for you, and one for you, and one for me. *Bon appetit!*"

Sierra gave Christy a look that said "Told you. We're wearing down all her defenses."

Christy took a bite of her truffle and began to chew it.

"No, no, no!" Marti scolded. "You don't chew a truffle! You let it dissolve slowly on your tongue. Savor the experience."

Sierra took a tiny bite of the rich chocolate and let it dissolve in her closed mouth. It was good. Very good.

"You're right," she said to Marti. "Make the moment last as long as you can."

"Chocolate should be a tender experience," Marti said. She closed her eyes and drew in a deep breath. "I can't remember the last time I had chocolate like this."

"Did Nelson bring you chocolates?" Sierra asked.

Marti slowly opened her eyes and looked down at her pastry bag, then over at Sierra. People were milling around the street, entering and exiting shops. It seemed as though everything clicked into slow motion as Marti said, "Nelson brought me anything I wanted, including chocolates."

"Whatever happened to him?" Christy ventured.

Sierra admired Christy's bravery. But then, how hard was it for Christy to step over a wall Sierra had just brought down?

It appeared the answer was on the edge of Marti's chocolate-smudged lips, as if she were about to divulge some secret. Then her lips closed, and she seemed to swallow more than her last bite of truffle.

"Perhaps I'll tell you sometime," she said in a hollow voice. Marti reached into her pastry bag and broke off a portion of the flaky croissant. She chewed it slowly, mechanically. Sierra couldn't tell whether Marti was savoring the pastry or if she had lost her taste for everything and was only going through the motions. It seemed to represent the way Sierra believed Marti went through life—making all the right moves without enjoying any of it.

They sat silently in the strong heat of the August sun, eating their pastries, each swept up in her own thoughts.

Chapter Twelve

*S*IERRA CHEWED HER PASTRY SLOWLY. SHE could feel the persistent sun on her face. Voices floated through the street. Overhead, she heard a bird call to its mate. The summer breeze blew across her bare legs, just lightly enough to make its presence known.

For many years, Sierra had compared the Holy Spirit to the wind, noting that it was always there, no matter how faint the breeze. The wind went where it wanted to go, and its path was easy to detect because it moved objects and people. But no one had ever seen the wind.

Sitting on the bench in Basel, Sierra felt that something deep inside her was coming alive. Was it desire? Passion? A sugar rush?

No, this was something emotional and spiritual blended together. The stirring was strong and vibrant. It made Sierra realize she wanted to enjoy to the absolute fullest this life God had given her. She wanted to be more aware of the Holy Spirit's "breeze" blowing through her life. She wanted its effects and presence to be evident in her. She knew she didn't want to turn out like Marti, living by schedules and goals, not tasting the sweetness that was before her.

Sierra realized that, lately, she had been setting up her life like Marti did. Sierra had rules, standards, goals for college. Her summer had been packed with working, volunteering at the homeless shelter, and being at church nearly every time the doors opened. For the first time, Sierra saw that she had organized a lot of the spontaneity and joy right out of life.

Then something else occurred to Sierra. She realized what her father had meant when he gave her the purity ring. He'd told her to enjoy herself. Sierra had all her goals in place, but where was the good clean fun in her life? This last-minute trip had awakened those impulses in her, and she liked it. This vitality felt good—freeing. And it felt right. Finally, Sierra was being true to who she was and who God had made her to be.

"What was that verse, Christy?"

Christy licked her fingers and wadded her empty pastry bag into a little ball. "Which verse? First Peter 1:8— the one Alex quoted yesterday?"

"Yes. What did it say about love?"

"I just read it in my Bible this morning and underlined it. It said, 'Above all, love each other deeply, because love covers over a multitude of sins.' "

"That's it," Sierra said. "Love each other deeply. How did Alex say it? Oh yeah, 'fervently.' " Sierra thought another moment and then said, "You do that, Christy. You love people fervently. I like that about you. I want to be like that."

Christy began to blush.

"You know what I don't understand?" Marti interjected. "How did you two become such good friends? When I was your age, Christy, I would never have enjoyed being friends with someone three years younger than myself. I certainly wouldn't have considered her to be a genuine friend."

"There's really only about two years difference between us," Christy said. "But it doesn't seem like even that much."

"It's because I'm so mature," Sierra said playfully in a deep voice.

Marti said, "I find that to be true."

"I was only kidding," Sierra said.

"I wasn't. You both are so much more aware of yourselves and of life than I was at your age. Mind you, I don't agree with the fervor of your Christianity, but I do think it's been an advantage for you both in some ways."

"It's not supposed to be an advantage," Christy said. "It's supposed to be my whole life."

"Oh, Christina! Can't you simply take the compliment without trying to correct me? I was being nice."

"I noticed that," Sierra commented.

Marti and Christy both looked at Sierra.

"I meant, I noticed you were being nice, Marti. I thought it was nice that you were complimenting us. Thank you."

"You're welcome. See, Christina? That's the proper way to respond to a compliment."

"I appreciate your comment, too," Christy said.

"Good," Marti said. She paused and then added, "I suppose we should get going. On to a dress shop?"

"How about a picnic?" Sierra asked.

"Isn't that what we just had?" Marti asked back.

"We picked up a map from the information booth," Christy said. "Sierra and I were thinking it would be fun to do some hiking and take a picnic snack up into the Alps."

"We're already taking a walk," Marti said, appearing unclear as to why a walk in the mountains would be more appealing than taking a stroll down this wonderful row of shops.

"Maybe tomorrow?" Christy asked hopefully.

"You'll have plenty of time to hike these mountains if you come to school here," Marti said, making her way into the crowds along the street.

Christy tossed her bag into a trash can. "Sierra won't."

"Sierra needs a dress," Marti said firmly. "We still haven't eaten at a really nice restaurant, and Sierra certainly won't be allowed in wearing those baggy shorts."

The rest of the afternoon was spent fulfilling Marti's goal of finding nice clothes for Sierra. They returned to the hotel by cab since they had walked so far and now had their arms loaded with bags.

"I'll ask the concierge to make reservations for us at seven," Marti announced as they entered the hotel lobby. "That gives you nearly two hours to rest, shower, and dress up. And do wear the black skirt, Sierra, not the gypsy one."

"Yes, Aunt Martha," Sierra teased in a nasal-sounding voice.

Marti turned sharply and gave Sierra an intensely disapproving look. Sierra knew she would never joke around like that again.

"Are you going to take a shower?" Sierra asked Christy as they tossed all their bags onto the beds.

"I'm thinking about it. You know what? I think my arms got sunburned. Can you believe that?"

"The sun was pretty hot when we were sitting in front of the bakery," Sierra said. "My cheeks feel red."

"They are a little," Christy said, examining Sierra's face. "How do you do that?"

"Do what?"

"You look perfectly fresh, like you don't need a shower at all. Your hair is perfect, and your face is perfect."

"My hair is never perfect. My hair has a mind of its own. It never cooperates with me," Sierra said, grabbing a handful of the long, unruly strands.

"Alex sure liked it," Christy teased. "Why don't you see if we got any phone messages?"

"You read my mind," Sierra said.

While Christy was in the shower, Sierra tried to figure out how to work the message retrieval service on the phone. An instruction sheet printed in German, English, French, and Italian was in the top drawer of the desk. It didn't help. Even the English instructions were hard to decipher. When Sierra finally pushed the right buttons, she was rewarded with the sound of Alex's deep voice on the other end.

"This is Alexander, and I am calling for See-hair-a. I will be at my cousin's house today helping him repair his automobile. If you do not already have arrangements for tomorrow, I would like to take you on a picnic. I will call again tonight, and we can make our plans. Ciao."

There was a click on the end of the receiver and a zing inside Sierra's heart. Alex hadn't forgotten about her. He wanted to take her on a picnic tomorrow. Or rather, to take Sierra and Christy on a picnic. Marti had to let them go. Sierra hoped Marti would be in a good mood at dinner when Sierra asked permission.

It was hard to distinguish what kind of mood Marti was in that evening. Sierra and Christy had dressed according to her instructions, both wearing basic black evening attire. They took their time putting on makeup and talking about Alex and the picnic. Christy urged Sierra to leave it up to her. She would find the right approach with her aunt.

Marti wore a stunning black dress with a string of pearls and black high heels. As the three of them paraded through the hotel lobby, Marti carried herself like a movie star at the Academy Awards. A cab was waiting for them and drove them to the nicest restaurant Sierra had ever been to in her life. The place was small and intimate. The light was golden, and the music from the string trio reverberated off the delicately painted ceiling.

Sierra noticed that everyone was dressed up, and everyone was wearing black. She leaned over once they were seated and softly thanked Marti for the new skirt. Then she asked Marti to please order for her since she trusted Marti's judgment more than her own at a place like this. Marti was pleased.

Their dinner was cold cucumber soup, veal with baby carrots that were arranged like a bouquet on her plate, and a swirl of garlicked mashed potatoes. And then coffee and dessert. Sierra thought dessert would be the perfect time to bring up the picnic with Alex. Christy and Sierra nibbled on a rich chocolate torte while Marti sipped her espresso in a dainty cup, which, according to Marti was called a "demitasse."

But Christy didn't say anything, so Sierra forced herself to wait until Christy decided the time was right.

They took the cab back to the hotel. The *alt stadt* was lit up beautifully at night, and many people were strolling on the bridge across the Rhine River or walking along the storefronts. Marti paid the cab driver, led the girls back upstairs, and in the hallway said good night to them.

"Oh," Christy said suddenly. "We haven't decided yet what we're going to do tomorrow. Would you like to come to our room so we can talk about it?"

"I thought we would go back to the school and meet with Mr. Pratt. We only have tomorrow," Marti reminded them. "The next day we have to leave."

"Oh," Christy said again.

"Is that our phone ringing?" Sierra said, pressing her ear to the door. "Hurry up! Open the door."

"Who would be calling you?" Marti said.

Sierra burst inside and reached for the phone. "Hello?"

"Is this See-hair-a?"

Just hearing Alex say her name with his distinctive accent brought a smile to her lips. "Yes, this is Sierra."

"This is Alex."

"Yes," Sierra said, trying to suppress a giggle, "I know."

"Did you receive my message?"

"Yes."

Christy was giving Sierra a "Well?" look.

"Who is it?" Marti asked.

"Would you like to go for a hike tomorrow?" Alex asked.

Sierra paused. "Yes, I would. But I'll need to talk to Marti about this."

"If it would be helpful, I will speak with her."

"Good idea."

Sierra held out the phone to Marti. "For you," she said, biting her lower lip and giving Christy a sideways glance.

"Hello? Who is this?" Marti asked. "Oh, yes, Alex. . . . What's that? . . . Tomorrow? I'm afraid we have plans already."

Sierra's heart sank.

"Why, yes, we are returning to the school. . . . No, in the morning." Then Marti was silent. To Sierra, it seemed like the longest pause in the world.

"Yes, all right then. . . . Thank you for calling. Good night."

Sierra watched Marti hang up and felt like diving to grab the phone. Sierra's stomach sank when she heard the "click" of the receiver.

Christy and Sierra waited with wide eyes.

"Well?" they asked in unison.

Chapter Thirteen

"**D**ID YOU TWO ARRANGE THIS?" MARTI asked with her hands on her hips.

"No," they said in one voice.

"You're telling me Alex decided on his own to call and invite you to go on a picnic?"

"Yes."

"He called earlier," Sierra explained. "While we were out shopping this afternoon. He left a message and said he would call back tonight. So, in a way, we did know about his invitation, but we didn't talk to him today."

"Why didn't you tell me he called earlier?" Marti asked.

"We're afraid of you," Sierra blurted out.

Marti let a rippling laugh escape. "Afraid of me? Why?"

"We really wanted to go," Christy explained. "We thought you might not agree unless we asked when you were in a good mood."

Marti lowered herself into the desk chair. "Is that what you think of me?"

"You haven't exactly been crazy about Alex," Sierra said.

She gave up all hope of seeing him again. Marti had responded so coolly on the phone, Sierra was certain Marti had ruined any possibility Sierra and Alex would get together.

"Your view of me is about to change." Marti slapped the top of the desk with her open palm. "Tomorrow morning at eight, we will meet downstairs for breakfast. At nine, Alex will take us to the school. After our meeting there, Alex will drop me off at an art festival in a small town not far from the school. He will then take the two of you out for a picnic lunch."

Sierra's heart soared. "That's great! Thank you!"

"See? I'm not such an old party pooper, after all. Now get some sleep. Tomorrow will be a busy day." With a swish, Marti left.

Sierra danced around the room. "I can't believe it! Your aunt has a streak of human kindness in her after all. This is going to be so great! A picnic in the hills! Is this going to be romantic, or what?"

"With me along, it'll probably be 'or what,' " Christy said. "I'm glad it worked out, though."

"Oh, yeah," Sierra said, reaching for her pillow to throw at Christy. "No thanks to you! When were you going to bring up the subject? On our plane ride home?"

"No," Christy said, ducking as the flying pillow came her way. "I was scared, just like you said. I've never admitted it before, but my aunt scares me sometimes. I like the way you get right at the heart of an issue and speak up truthfully. I have a hard time doing that."

"It gets me in lots of trouble," Sierra said.

"Not tonight, it didn't."

"Christy," Sierra said, flopping onto her stomach across the bed, "do you think it's right for me to be so excited about seeing Alex?"

"Of course. Why do you even ask?"

"Because I don't usually get all hyper about seeing a guy. It's weird. I mean, where could this relationship possibly lead? I probably won't ever see him again after tomorrow."

"Hold that thought. I'll be right back." Christy slipped off her shoes and grabbed her pajamas.

While Christy was in the bathroom, Sierra let her thoughts fly freely. When Christy returned in her pajamas, Sierra asked, "Did you ever go out with a guy only one time and that was it? I mean, was there ever an Alex in your life?"

"Sort of." Christy fluffed up her pillow and got comfy on the bed. "I was a counselor at camp one summer, and this guy, Jaeson, asked me to go out with him one night. Well, he didn't exactly tell me where we were going. He just asked me to go to a movie. I went, but once we had left our camp area, he took my hand and said he was going to teach me how to paddle a canoe."

Sierra let out a hoot. "Now that's an original line! Did you like this guy?"

"Yes, sort of, I think. Now, it seems unbelievable that I

ever liked him, but I know I had strong feelings for him then. Looking back, though, I don't know if I ever really liked Jaeson or if I just liked the attention he gave me."

Sierra's emotions began to plummet. What if she were just after the attention? Earlier that summer, she'd gone through that with Drake, a guy from school. After their first and only date, she had decided she liked the *idea* of someone asking her out more than she liked actually having a relationship. There were too many complications in trying to define the relationship, especially trying to define it to her friends.

But Christy didn't seem to have any problem with Sierra and Alex's relationship. It was strange—when Drake had entered the picture, all of Sierra's friendships became strained. But now, having Alex around hadn't changed Sierra and Christy's friendship at all.

Christy continued. "I'm not saying I'm sorry I went out on the lake with Jaeson. It was beautiful the way the moon rose and shone across the water. Jaeson had set up the canoe with a candle and flowers. And he had peanut butter cookies he had saved from the first night of camp. It was all very sweet of him."

"Did you have permission to be away from the campers?" Sierra asked.

"No. And I've always felt bad about that part. It wasn't right that we sneaked out. No one found out, but it didn't matter. Leaving the main meeting was against the rules, and we could have gotten into trouble. It bothered me for a long time. I asked God for forgiveness, and then I even wrote a letter to the camp dean to confess. He wrote me a very nice letter back, but to this day I still feel bad about breaking the rules."

Sierra was glad she hadn't sneaked out to see Alex. She didn't have to, because everything was working out. She knew what Christy meant, though. Sierra would have felt bad for a long time, too.

"Can I ask the big question?"

"You want to know if Jaeson taught me how to paddle the canoe correctly? Yes, as a matter of fact, he did."

"No," Sierra laughed, "you know that's not what I was going to ask."

Christy's lips turned up in a smile. "Did Jaeson kiss me?"

"Well, did he?"

"No." Christy looked off toward the ceiling with both arms behind her head. "I remember being so nervous. I thought he was going to kiss me, and then he reached over and brushed my cheek. But it was only because I had cookie crumbs stuck there. I must have looked like such a dork to him."

"I'm sure that's not what he thought."

Christy turned onto her side and propped her head up with her arm. "You know what I think? I think a lot of things aren't about what we think they're about. Like the canoe ride. It wasn't about Jaeson, our relationship, or us kissing or not kissing. What I remember most about that night—besides that big, fat, yellow moon and the way it came over the mountain—was that Jaeson asked me what my dream was. That's what that whole night was really about."

Christy sat up and gave her full attention to Sierra. "Jaeson asked me, 'What's your dream?' and I told him something I'd never told anyone else before."

Sierra sat up and waited, feeling honored to share in Christy's secret.

"Wow," Christy said in a moment of sudden revelation, "I haven't thought of this in ages. I told him my dream was to go to Europe. I said I wanted to visit a real castle and go for a gondola ride in Venice."

"That's what you told him?"

Christy nodded. "Isn't that wild? I had no idea then that I'd go to Europe twice in one year, or actually live in a castle like we did in England."

"Guess all that's left is the gondola ride," Sierra said. She could feel her sunburned cheeks tightening as she flashed Christy a big smile. "Kind of a God-thing that you remembered your dreams of Europe tonight, when you have to decide about the school."

Christy nodded solemnly. "I know. It is. Maybe God has been preparing me for this school for a long time, and it isn't such a whim after all."

They shared a comfortable silence before Sierra spoke up again. "Do you think your relationship with Jaeson was about your dreams and not about building a lasting friendship?"

"Something like that," Christy said slowly. "That night was about me being brave enough to open my heart and tell my dream to Jaeson. To be honest, it doesn't really matter now whether or not I kissed him. As long as it was only a quick, innocent kiss. It would have mattered if we had, you know, done more. Then I would have been giving away part of my passion, and I want to save all my passion for just one man."

"Todd," Sierra answered for her.

"My husband, whoever he will be. I haven't given my passionate, intimate self to Todd—or to any guy. I've only kissed a few guys, but to me a short, tender kiss is way different from a passionate embrace and prolonged, heart-and-soul kissing. You know what I mean?"

"Not from personal experience, but yes, I think I understand. I never thought of it that way before. I thought the goal was to not kiss at all until you're standing at the wedding altar, like Doug and Tracy did."

"That's what was right for them," Christy said. "Doug is such a loving and affectionate guy. You know how he is, always hugging everyone. I think it would have been hard for him to only give a girlfriend a short, sweet kiss. And I think he knew that, too. He set a very high standard, and I totally admire him for sticking to it."

"So, what you're saying is that you and Todd have a different standard, but you think that's okay?" Sierra was trying to understand.

"Yes, I do. Todd and I have drawn the line at light kissing. We hug and hold hands, too. But that's it. And that's all it'll be for me until I marry, no matter whom I end up with. Todd told me one time that his goal was to give me his affection but not his passion. That made sense to me and that's where I draw the line, too. For us, affection can mean brief kisses. For someone else, that might be too big of a temptation or something."

Sierra was listening carefully to Christy's words. She knew it was wise advice. Their talk made Sierra think of her friend back home, Amy, who had told Sierra about a first date she'd had with a guy from work. Amy had said proudly that they had made out in his car for a long time.

When Sierra got home from this trip, she planned to have a lengthy conversation with Amy. She wanted to tell Amy some of the things Christy had just said. It would be better to talk with Amy than to judge her, which was the way Sierra had first reacted. Amy had gotten mad and defensive. Their whole friendship seemed to turn upside down in one conversation. Now Sierra was determined to find a way to make things right.

Sierra smiled at Christy. "I really appreciate your sharing with me, Christy. It's good to be able to talk to someone who has been there and has it figured out," she said.

Christy laughed. "I wish I had the rest of my life figured out! I'm glad we can talk about all this stuff, too. You help me a lot with your insights—especially when it comes to my aunt. I'll be honest with you: I didn't know how well this trip would go."

"I had my doubts, too," Sierra said as she started to get ready for bed.

"It's going much better than I thought," Christy said,

slipping underneath her covers.

"There's always tomorrow," Sierra said. She turned out the light. "It's a fresh new day with more note-card racks to send crashing to the ground."

Christy started to laugh. "I couldn't believe that happened!"

Sierra laughed, too. "We should be safe in the wide open trails of the Black Forest. You can never be completely sure, though. I'll probably knock over a cow or something."

Christy kept laughing.

They whispered and giggled like 10-year-olds at a sleepover until they were too drowsy to talk. Sierra never slept better.

Chapter Fourteen

The next morning, specks of rain dotted the windshield as Alex drove the three women to the Black Forest People's School. A wreath of frothy mist hung over the green hills before them. Sierra tried hard not to worry that their picnic might be canceled.

Alex seemed to read her thoughts. "It is only the morning dew," he said, turning on the windshield wipers. "It will be clear before we go on our hike."

"If it doesn't clear up," Marti said, "you can come to the art festival with me. Alex tells me it's the largest in this region."

"It will clear," Alex said.

They arrived right on time at the school. While Christy and Marti met with Mr. Pratt, Sierra and Alex sat on a cushioned bench in the alcove of the school's entrance. Sierra decided at once that she liked this romantic setting. The polished wood floor reflected the massive light fixture that hung from the center of the rounded ceiling. The light looked like the top of a tree that had been cut off in winter, bronzed, and then adorned with rows of flickering candles on its frozen, outstretched limbs. The double doors to their left each had an oval in the center filled with a mosaic of clear, beveled glass. The morning light shone through the glass, creating lacy patterns at their feet.

Every word Alex and Sierra spoke echoed off the ceiling. They lowered their voices and spoke in hushed tones.

"We have much to talk of," Alex said, his deep voice still echoing through the room.

Sierra smiled. "Are you going to ask me about my dreams?"

Alex wrinkled his forehead. "Your dreams?" he questioned.

"Never mind," Sierra said. "What was it you wanted to talk about?"

Sierra noticed that Alex's dark hair was less co-operative than usual today. Instead of staying straight back with only one runaway clump, all his hair fell freely. It made him look like an Olympic skier who, upon completing his run, had pulled off his cap at the victory line. Sierra liked the look.

"What will you do when you return home?" Alex asked.

"I don't know," Sierra answered. Home was the last thing on her mind. "Work some extra hours, I guess, and get ready for school."

"This is your final year?"

Sierra nodded. "My senior year."

"And what will you then do?"

"Do you mean after I graduate from high school?"

"Yes. Then what?"

Sierra shrugged. "Go to college somewhere. I don't know where."

"I was told by an American that you must know these things early because some universities are difficult to enter."

"Some are. But I need to give it more thought."

Alex nodded his agreement. "More thought and more prayer. Am I right?"

He had been sitting only a few inches from Sierra, with his right arm resting on the back of the bench. He wasn't touching her, but she almost felt he was, since he was so close to, and focused on, her. Now he adjusted his position slightly, and for a moment his hand brushed against her shoulder.

Put your arm all the way around me and draw me close, Alex. I want you to.

Sierra's thoughts surprised her. But they felt natural. She remembered what Christy had said the previous night and wondered if she was feeling affection or passion. *Or is affection the beginning of passion?* Sierra asked herself. Then she had another mysterious thought: *What if I'm the kind of person who can't restrain myself and express only affection? What if my passions suddenly overpower me? Is that what happened to Amy on her date with Nathan?*

Sierra forced her thoughts back into the conversation.

"Oh, um, yes. Pray about my future," she said. "You're right. I need to do more praying and to start planning. This whole summer went by way too fast. . . . What about you? When will you find out if you can get into the university?"

"Perhaps the letter will be waiting when I return home in two weeks." Alex's high cheekbones seemed to lift even more as a smile crossed his lips. "You should have known me last winter. I could not eat or sleep because of my worry over being accepted to the university. Now I have completely changed."

Sierra wasn't sure she understood what Alex was saying. "Do you mean you aren't worried about getting into the university anymore?"

"Worry," Alex repeated thoughtfully. "I have changed my views on worry. Do you know the German word for *worry* is the same as 'strangle'?"

"Is it really?"

Alex took both his hands and grabbed himself around the neck, demonstrating being strangled.

Sierra laughed softly. Her laughter echoed off the high ceiling.

"You have such a song in your laughter. I'm beginning to know this song, and it brings me a good feeling." Alex reached over and took Sierra's hand.

She thought her heart would stop.

"There are songs all around us," he said, smoothing his fingers over the top of her hand. "Even in the touch of two friends. Shh. Listen. Do you hear the music our hands are making?"

Sierra definitely heard something. But it sounded more like bass drums pounding in her ears. She imagined it was her heart, but maybe it was music, music she was not used to yet. She smiled at Alex and said, "Tell me what you hear."

Alex closed his eyes and tilted back his head, resting it against the wood-paneled wall of their private alcove. He drew in a deep breath and squeezed Sierra's hand more tightly. "I hear the sound a river makes going over rocks on its way to the sea." Then softly he added, "There is a river of life in you, See-hair-a. See-hair-a of the mountains, not of the desert."

She felt relaxed as he spoke, comfortable holding his hand and absorbing his poetic words. She looked down at their hands, clasped together and resting on her leg. Right above their hands was the ivy-leaf-shaped mustard stain on her jeans.

I don't think I'll ever wash these jeans again.

"What do you hear?" Alex asked without opening his eyes.

Sierra closed her eyes and leaned back her head. The hall was silent for a moment. "I don't know what I hear." Nothing she said would be able to match Alex's poetic words.

"Listen," Alex urged her. His voice was barely a whisper. His touch on her hand was light.

Sierra listened. She still didn't hear anything poetic. But she felt something. "I feel happy," Sierra said.

"Happy," Alex repeated. "One does not always feel this

in life. Especially where I live. You are not choked with worry. This is good."

Down the hall they could hear voices. Marti, Christy, and Mr. Pratt were headed their way. Sierra didn't want their private time to end. She wondered if she should let go of Alex's hand or if he would let go of hers.

He stood, bringing her up with him, and then he let go of her hand. Not quickly, as though he didn't want to be seen by Mr. Pratt and the others. Alex lingered as he let go.

"Well?" Sierra asked Christy. "What did you decide about school?"

Christy looked at Mr. Pratt and then at Marti. When neither of them answered, she spoke up. "I called my parents and talked to them about everything."

"And?"

Christy nodded slowly. "I'm going to come here. I've made a year's commitment."

"Isn't that marvelous?" Marti asked. "Studying abroad is going to be fabulous for Christy. Don't you agree, Sierra?"

Sierra tried to read Christy's expression. She seemed happy and at peace with her choice.

"It's great," Sierra said. "I think you're going to have some incredible experiences."

Christy nodded. "I'm worried about a few things, but I think they'll work out."

"Don't worry," Alex said, repeating his strangling demonstration. "It will choke you."

Christy looked at Sierra for an explanation. "We'll tell you all about it on our picnic."

An hour later, Alex was leading Christy and Sierra along a dirt trail up the side of a hill. Marti had appeared to be content spending the afternoon taking in the art festival. She had left them cheerfully and asked them to be back in two hours.

"I was correct about the weather, was I not?" Alex said, pausing to survey the landscape.

The blue August sky willingly shared its open spaces with a host of plump and lazy clouds. All around them, a blanket of vibrant green grass covered the lumpy earth. To their right, a tangle of wild berry bushes kept the last of their summer treasure tucked inside their thorny caverns.

They had passed half a dozen cows on their climb up the mountain. Each cow wore a large bell around its neck, which played an enchanting strain of music as the cow grazed. Christy said she thought the cows were "cuter" than the cows at home, and Alex laughed. She told him she was qualified to make this distinction because her father was a dairy farmer, and she had spent the first 15 years of her life around cows.

Sierra drew in a deep breath. "The air is so rich here, and I love this view! I'm so glad we came. Hiking is my favorite hobby. It does something to my spirit to rise above the rest of the world," she said in satisfaction.

"I love it here, too," Christy said. "And it's so close to the school. I can't believe I'll be able to come up here any time I want. This is gorgeous!"

"Where would you like to have our picnic?" Alex asked.

"Right here," Sierra said. "This view is beautiful."

"Then we stop here."

Alex led them a few feet off the trail onto the grass. All three of them removed their day packs and pulled out their offerings for the picnic.

"I hope you are not too hungry," Alex said. "I did not bring a lot, and it is not specialty food."

"Don't worry about it," Sierra said. "We were more interested in the hike than the picnic. The food is a bonus."

"A bonus?" Alex repeated.

"It's extra," Sierra said, defining the unfamiliar word. "Besides, Christy and I have a few goodies to share, too."

"Two candy bars," Christy said, cleaning out her day pack and placing the food in front of them.

"I have an orange left over from breakfast," Sierra said.

"Something here to drink," said Alex. "And some cheese and bread." He pulled out a pocket knife and sliced off a hunk of cheese from the block in his hand, offering it to Sierra on the blade of his knife.

"It's practically a feast," Christy said when she accepted the next wedge of cheese Alex cut. "Now, are you going to tell me what the strangling was about at school? You kind of made me nervous."

"Alex did that when you said you were worried," Sierra explained. She broke off a corner from the loaf of bread resting on top of Alex's pack and explained how Alex had been worried about getting into the university. "We're not supposed to worry, because worry strangles us."

"I sure don't want to go through life feeling strangled." Christy reached for the bread with her free hand. She couldn't pull off a corner, so Alex held on to the loaf, and she broke off the bread with his help.

Sierra looked around at the perfect day. "Doesn't it seem as though we've stepped into a picture?" she asked. The breeze lifted the loose side strands of her hair and playfully brushed them across her face. "Christy, you have to make this your thinking spot. It's so beautiful."

"I know," Christy said, drinking in the view with Sierra. "I'm getting kind of excited about coming to school here. Can you imagine how pretty this is all going to be in winter? I haven't seen much snow since we left Wisconsin. This might be my first white Christmas in five years."

Alex stretched out on his side and leaned on his arm. He reclined on the grass as if he didn't have a care in the world. "I've never known Christmas without snow," he said. "I much prefer this sunshine." He reached over and brushed the side of Sierra's bare arm with the top of his fingers. "The way the sun makes your skin warm like this, I like very much." He drew his hand back and broke off another chunk of bread.

Sierra closed her eyes and listened. What was that? She heard something. Maybe it was the distant chiming of the cows' bells or the birds singing in the trees. Whatever it was, when Alex touched her arm, she definitely heard music.

Chapter Fifteen

"**I**T WAS MORE THAN A FUN PICNIC," Sierra explained to Marti as Alex drove them back to the hotel. "For me, it was a spiritual experience."

Marti laughed bluntly. "You know, my dear Sierra, I do believe you and my niece could manage to make a spiritual experience out of washing your hair. You mustn't become so absorbed with your heavenly thoughts, or you will be of no earthly good to anyone."

Sierra glanced at Christy, who gave a silent signal to let Marti's comment go. From the moment they had picked her up at the art festival, she had seemed a little wobbly in her movements. Apparently, the festival offered an abundance of wine-tasting opportunities, of which Marti took advantage. And when Sierra heard the way Marti slurred the word "experience," Sierra was almost certain that Marti had tasted too much wine.

"What are you doing tonight?" Alex asked.

"We must pack," Marti said. "Sierra and Christy will not be available for dinner because we have plans."

"May I offer you a ride to the train in the morning?"

"Yes, you may," said Marti. "We must leave the hotel at seven o'clock. Will you pick us up?"

"Yes," Alex said. "I will be there at seven."

He pulled up in front of the hotel just as giant drops of rain began to splash against the windshield.

"That was convenient," Marti said. "Now I suppose you will think the rain coming back after your picnic is also spiritual."

None of them commented. Alex got out first and opened the door for Marti. Sierra and Christy climbed out and stood under the front canopy. The rain sounded like rapid-fire pellets on the overhang.

"It's really coming down," Sierra said.

"Thanks again for everything, Alex," Christy said. "We'll see you in the morning."

"Yes. At seven. I will be here."

He turned to Sierra and gave her a warm smile. For several seconds, they looked into each other's eyes, neither of them speaking. Then Alex wrapped his arms around Sierra and hugged her close. She wasn't expecting it and took a moment to respond before hugging him back.

Alex pulled away, brushing his chin against the side of her hair. "*Tschuss,*" he said.

Sierra assumed he was saying good-bye in German or French or maybe a combination of both languages.

"Bye. I'll see you tomorrow."

He turned to dash back to his car. The rain was coming

down so hard and loud, it seemed the canopy above them would burst open. A sudden flash of lightning lit up the sky, followed by a loud boom of thunder.

"Hurry," Marti called to the girls. "Hurry inside!" She looked panicked.

The second flash of lightning struck just as Sierra unlocked the door to their room. The lights in the hallway flickered. Three seconds later, the thunder came.

"This is not good," Marti said, following the girls into their room. "Don't turn on your television, and stay away from the windows."

"We used to have powerful thunderstorms like this in the mountains where I grew up," Sierra said. "I'm sure this storm is much more dramatic than the kind of storms you get at the beach where you live."

Marti didn't look comforted. She slipped off her shoes and made herself at home on Sierra's bed. "Wouldn't you know?" Marti said, shaking her head. "Now I wish Robert were here."

Sierra realized this was the first time during the entire trip that Marti had mentioned her husband. "Why didn't he come?" Sierra asked.

"Because of his face, of course," Marti answered bluntly. Recovering quickly from her brashness, she added, "What I mean to say is, his scars are still healing from the burns, and he shouldn't travel until after the plastic surgery is completed. He looks terrible. You know. You've seen him. Both of you. Do you think he should be traveling?"

Sierra could tell the alcohol was affecting Marti's judgment. Ordinarily, she would never be so frank about her husband. Could it be she was so obsessed with appearances that she was embarrassed by Bob's? It had only been five months since the gas barbecue accident had burned the side of his face, his neck, and his ear. Sierra didn't know much about burns, but she guessed Bob wouldn't be "presentable" by Marti's standards for a long time.

"Well? Do you think he should be traveling?" Marti again asked for an answer.

"I guess it depends on what the doctor recommends," Christy stated diplomatically.

"Doctors don't know anything," Marti muttered. "They said they could fix my baby, but they couldn't. They said they could fix me, but they couldn't. Why should I believe them when they say they can fix my husband?"

Sierra carefully glanced at Christy, who was seated on the edge of her bed. Christy seemed as startled as Sierra that Marti had so casually mentioned her baby. The great secret was out.

Another flash of lightning, trailed by roaring thunder, caused them to jump. Sierra sat down on the end of her bed and faced Marti. She decided if she was going to play detective about Marti's past, this was the moment.

"What happened to your baby?" Sierra said, trying to sound casual.

Marti blinked several times. "You know about Johanna?"

"I do," Christy said, moving over to Sierra's bed and closing the small circle. "Mom told me a few years ago. I'm really sorry she died. I wish you would have told me about her, Aunt Marti."

"What good would that have done?"

"It would have helped me to know you better."

"Ha!" Marti laughed. "There's a lot you don't know about me. I was never like you, all open and sweet. I had secrets. Secrets hardly anyone else knew."

"You don't have to tell us if you don't want to," Christy said. Her voice was full of compassion.

Marti drew in a deep breath through her nose. "No, I think you're old enough now. I promised myself I'd tell you one day. I suppose today is as good as any day. Your mother knows, but I asked her not to tell you because I thought you should hear it from me."

Sierra felt out of place. Here she had seen herself on a great mission to get Marti to open up to them. Now that she was about to talk, it seemed her confession should be between herself and Christy. Sierra didn't belong.

"Do you want me to go into your room while you and Christy talk?" Sierra asked Marti.

Another round of lightning and thunder punctuated the end of Sierra's sentence with a loud bang.

"You might as well hear this, too. You probably already have figured out most of it," Marti said, turning her attention to Sierra. Marti's right eyelid seemed to droop slightly. Her usually sophisticated air was gone. "You don't miss a thing, do you, Sierra? No one your age should be as smart as you."

Sierra didn't know if she had been insulted or complimented. She leaned back and decided it would probably be best if she didn't say anything.

"Well? Go ahead and tell my niece. She hasn't figured it out yet," Marti said to Sierra.

"Figured out what?" Sierra said. "I really don't know what you mean."

"Johanna. Tell her about how Johanna was Nelson's child."

A wave of nausea hit Sierra. She didn't know why she had thought it would be cool to unlock Marti's psyche.

Marti began her story. "We were in love. Very, very much in love when we started dating. I was 15. That's why I wanted you to come stay with me the summer you turned 15, Christy. I wanted to warn you about what can happen to nice girls who know nothing about men and life. I knew nothing when I was your age."

Marti shook her head and fixed her gaze on her niece. "But you were so different from me. I didn't know how to tell you. I didn't want to make you grow up fast like I did, so I didn't say anything."

An uneasy silence followed. It was as if they were waiting for the lightning and thunder to shatter the intensity of the moment.

"What happened?" Christy finally asked in a small, tight voice.

"I got pregnant when I was 17. I told Nelson, and I honestly expected him to marry me. But he left town. I never saw him again."

"That must have been awful for you," Christy said.

"I went to live with your parents, Christy. I told everyone it was because my older sister was pregnant, and she needed my help. No one knew I was pregnant, too. The baby came early and was, well . . . she was less than whole. I knew God was punishing me. But I didn't understand why He had to punish an innocent baby. Right after little Johanna died, your mother went into labor. I somehow felt responsible for that, too, because of the burden I'd placed on Margaret. You were born the next day, Christina, and you were perfect."

The lights in their room flickered again and then went out. It was early evening, but the storm raging outside made everything turn dark.

"I have a flashlight," Sierra said, reaching for her day pack on the floor.

"Is this one of your God-things, Christy?" Marti said with a bite to her waning voice. "This sudden darkness makes for an added touch, doesn't it? Dark—that's how I felt the day you were born. My sister was God's favored one, and I, the terrible sinner, was cursed. I moved to California and worked hard to put myself through secretarial school. My first job was for your uncle, Bob. He fell in love with me and accepted me as I was. All I wanted was someone to love me and to have a daughter of our own."

Marti seemed to be running out of energy as she finished her story. "But your God doesn't forget, does He? I was diagnosed as infertile. The doctor said he could fix me, but he couldn't. You can't fight God, can you?"

"Sure you can," Sierra said. "You can fight Him and blame Him and be mad at Him all you want. He's still God. He's still in control of everything that happens. He still loves you."

Marti made a snorting sound. "Well, He has a very strange way of showing it."

In the dull light of their room, Sierra couldn't quite make out Christy's expression. The beam from the flashlight was directed toward the bathroom, creating elongated shadows across the wall.

"He does love you," Christy added to Sierra's words.

Marti shook her head. "Love," she said. "You two have no idea what love is. You don't know what I'm talking about at all. If God is so loving and protective, then He's going to have to prove it to me." Marti leaned forward and, with some difficulty, tried to stand. She bent over to pick up her shoes and then stood up, her legs wobbling.

"Now you know, Christina. Your aunt is a horrible person, and God has given up on her. I suppose I should be glad you are such a good girl and He has smiled on you."

"God never gives up on anyone," Christy said, rising from the bed and taking quick steps in the darkness to stand beside her aunt. Christy put her arms around Marti and said fervently, "I love you, Aunt Marti. I'm sorry you have gone through such horrible things in your life. My love for you won't ever change. And I think you know deep down that God hasn't given up on you. He's just waiting for you to come to Him."

Marti received only a bit of the hug. She pulled away, and straightening up, she mumbled, "Well, He'll just have to keep waiting for me because I have a suitcase to pack and a train to catch in the morning."

With that, she took unsteady steps into her room and shut the door in exact unison with a vicious clap of thunder.

Chapter Sixteen

"CHRISTY, ARE YOU AWAKE?" SIERRA WHISPERED in the darkness of their hotel room.

They had gone to bed hours earlier. After Marti had left, they had ordered room service for dinner and packed their belongings while they discussed the intense conversation with Marti. The storm had continued outside, and now the noise of the pelting rain had awakened Sierra.

Christy didn't answer.

Rats! She's asleep. I wish I could fall back to sleep.

Sierra also wished Marti would have been more open to what Christy had said about how Marti needed to come to God. That's what had happened to Bob after the barbecue accident. For years, he had told Christy he didn't need God, but after the accident, he had done a complete turnaround. In the hospital, Bob had surrendered his life to Christ. The transformation had been instantaneous and obvious.

Sierra suspected Marti had not only turned a cold shoulder to God, but had also done the same to her husband now that he was a Christian.

Long into the stormy night, Sierra prayed. So much had happened in the past few days, and each of these events had been significant.

The rain pounded against their windows. The wind made a shrill, piercing noise that filled the dark room.

The clamorous storm reminded Sierra of the verse Alex had read in 1 Peter: "The end of all things is at hand; therefore be serious and watchful in your prayers. Above all things have fervent love for one another, for 'love will cover a multitude of sins.'" Sierra shuddered.

Now that she better understood Marti, Sierra wished she hadn't prejudged the woman so severely. Christy had done the right thing. She had loved her aunt unconditionally. Sierra closed her eyes and prayed for God to teach her that kind of love.

But by seven o'clock the next morning, her commitment to unconditional love was being tested. Marti was not feeling well. She yelled at Sierra and Christy for taking too long to get down to the lobby. Alex was there waiting for them, but when he greeted them, Marti acted as if she had never agreed to let Alex take them to the train station. She insisted he put down their luggage. They would take a cab. Alex could go home.

Marti's moodiness was driving Sierra crazy. She tried to face each of Marti's mood swings calmly, like Christy did. But when Marti started being downright mean to Alex, Sierra had to defend him.

"Yesterday you said you wanted Alex to take us to the

train station," she said, giving Marti a hard look. "He went to all the trouble to come get us—don't you think we should go with him?"

Marti glared right back at Sierra. "Oh, I don't care!" she said at last. "Do whatever you want. I see that my opinion is of no value."

"I'll help you carry our stuff to the car," Sierra said to Alex. "Where are you parked?"

Alex led the way while Sierra followed with Christy. Marti trailed behind.

"Please don't let her get to you," Sierra said to Alex. "I'm sorry she treated you that way."

"This is not your responsibility," Alex said. "There is no need for you to apologize. I think the battle in her heart is very strong."

Sierra nodded. Alex understood what was going on, perhaps even better than Christy or Sierra did.

They drove through the rain-drenched streets to the Badisher Bahnhof. A steady drizzle was coming from the gray clouds that hung over them, and the drab light muted the bright colors that had sparkled on these streets only the day before. A warm yellow light glowed inside the bakery, but all the other stores appeared dreary, like the day.

"Do you have your tickets already?" Alex asked.

"Of course we do," Marti snapped. "The minute we get to the station, I want this luggage loaded onto the train, and I want you girls to go immediately to your seats."

"Okay," Christy agreed.

Sierra was thinking of how she was going to say good-bye to Alex. He had made such an impact on her in the short time they had been together. She knew she had become a different person, partly because of him. Sierra needed to tell that to Alex. She wanted to say it privately, face-to-face, so that she could look into his dark eyes one more time.

She and Christy had been late arriving in the lobby that morning because Sierra had gone back to the room to write her address on a piece of hotel stationery. She wanted to find the right moment to give Alex that piece of paper. With that in mind, Sierra knew she couldn't promise Marti she would board the train the instant they got there. So Sierra kept quiet.

They pulled up in front of the station. Sierra was glad to see the two lions were still there, guarding the entrance and reminding her of Narnia and of Christ. She prayed silently, asking God to provide a chance for her to say good-bye to Alex the way she wanted to, the way she felt she must.

Entering the station with them, Alex carted their luggage to track number seven, where their train was beginning to board passengers.

Marti rummaged through her purse and checked the papers in her hand. "My ticket!" she squawked in a panic. "I've lost my ticket! Here's Christy's and Sierra's, but mine is gone."

"Have you checked in your bags?" Alex asked.

"It's not in there!"

"Maybe we should check," Christy suggested, bending to unzip the top of Marti's suitcase.

"It's locked," Marti snapped. "Here, let me do that."

"I'll check in the car," Alex offered.

"And I'll go with him," Sierra blurted out. She was beginning to feel panicked, too. Not about the tickets, but about the possibility of never seeing Alex again. What if she could never tell him the words that were on her heart?

Before Marti could object, Sierra and Alex were dashing through the train station on their way to the car. Alex quickly unlocked it and began to look under the seats, while Sierra went through the backseat and checked the glove compartment.

"I don't see it," she said.

"I do not either. Maybe they have found it in the suitcase. We must go back before the train leaves."

Alex locked the car, and they began to run back to track number seven.

When they arrived at the front of the long train, both of them were breathing hard. They couldn't find Marti or Christy among the dozens of people standing along the platform. A young couple was saying good-bye, wrapped in each other's arms. That was how Sierra had wanted to say good-bye to Alex, but now everything was too frenzied.

"Where did they go?" Sierra asked, panting.

"Perhaps they found the ticket and boarded the train," Alex suggested.

"They wouldn't go without me!"

"Perhaps they think you will get on when you do not see them."

Sierra looked right and left. There wasn't a trace of Marti and Christy anywhere.

"What should I do, Alex?"

"I think perhaps you should get on the train. You will not otherwise make it to the airport to take your flight home."

Forgetting all her plans to give Alex a tender farewell and to slip her address into his hand, Sierra put her foot on the first step into the train and grabbed the handrail. She paused. Something wasn't right. Her heart began to race the way it had on the airplane when she had the nightmare about crashing.

Sierra turned for one last look.

"Good-bye, See-hair-a," Alex called out, lifting his arm to her as if offering a benediction. "May God be with you always."

A loud bell chimed, and the train lurched forward. Sierra knew she needed to move inside, but she couldn't force herself to go further onto the train.

From somewhere down the platform, Sierra heard her name being called. The train made a hissing noise and began to pull slowly out of the station.

"Alex," Sierra cried, "I think I heard Christy. On the platform!"

Alex began to walk fast, keeping pace with Sierra as the train moved forward. He looked down the platform and then back at Sierra. "It is her! Christy comes! Jump,

See-hair-a! I will catch you."

All the feelings of terror that had started in her racing heart now exploded into her stomach and throat, paralyzing her.

"You must jump!" Alex called. "I will catch you! Now!"

Sierra held her breath and jumped into Alex's waiting arms.

Chapter Seventeen

SIERRA COLLIDED WITH ALEX'S CHEST. THE impact made it impossible for him to stay standing. In one great tumbling motion, he fell to the ground, his arms tightly wrapped around Sierra as she came down with him.

"Ouch!" Sierra yelped.

"Ooof," was all Alex could manage.

"Are you all right?" Sierra asked, trying to get up off the ground.

Alex's eyes were wide. His mouth moved, but no sound came out.

"Oh, no!" Sierra said, reaching for his hand. "I hurt you, didn't I?"

Alex tried to force out a word, but instead he coughed a deep, long cough. Behind them the last few train cars were leaving the station, and the noise went with them.

"Sierra!" Christy cried, arriving beside them and kneeling down next to her friends. "Are you guys okay? I saw you jump. I thought you were going to die!"

"I think Alex almost did die," Sierra said.

She and Christy both helped him to sit up. His hair was pushed forward in his eyes. He shook his head and drew in a deep breath.

"It is all right," he said at last. "The air went from me."

"Oh, I am so sorry!" Sierra said. "I shouldn't have jumped so hard. I didn't mean to knock you over. I'm so sorry."

"It is all right," Alex said shakily and rose to his feet.

"Christy, where were you?" Sierra asked. "We didn't see you or Marti anywhere. I thought you must have boarded the train."

"We were down there." Christy pointed. "Marti's sitting on a bench, and our luggage is on a cart. Maybe it was blocking your view of us. We were right where you left us, but I think you came in a different entrance, at the other end of the train."

"Did you find the ticket?" Sierra asked as they began to walk toward Marti. "Not that it matters. We just missed the train."

"No," Christy said, "we can't find the ticket anywhere. My aunt is about to blow a mainspring, as my dad always says. That's why I had her sit on the bench."

"I'm sorry to do this to you, Christy," Sierra moaned.

"Don't worry about it. It's definitely not your fault. I told Aunt Marti that God was in control, and we shouldn't worry. You know, it strangles people." Christy imitated Alex's strangling demonstration.

"What did Marti say?"

"She just about strangled me, so I didn't say anything else."

"Wise choice."

"Then it was so strange," Christy said. "I was sitting there on the bench with her, and all of a sudden I looked up, and way down at the end of the track I saw your day pack and all your blond hair, Sierra. I knew it was you."

"I'm glad you saw me," Sierra said.

"Me, too."

They arrived at the bench where Marti was seated with her arms tightly drawn across her middle. The scowl on her face was bitter.

The worst part was, Marti didn't say a word. Sierra expected to have to defend herself in a long yelling match. Marti, however, did not throw the first punch. She just sat there, staring at them as if they were responsible for the problems.

"May I make a suggestion?" Alex said calmly, having finally caught his breath. "Perhaps we can check at the ticket desk to see if they have you on their computer. They can issue you a new ticket, and you can board the very next train."

This suggestion did not appeal to Marti. She wouldn't move. She wouldn't speak.

"We have to do something," Christy said. "Would you like it if I went to check on the tickets, and you could stay here?"

"No!" Marti stated emphatically. "I am not letting either of you out of my sight for another second. We will all go. Alex, get the luggage."

Of all the things Marti had said, her insulting

command to Alex angered Sierra the most. Marti could say whatever she wanted to Sierra, and it wouldn't really matter. Sierra knew none of the mix-up was her fault. After all, they were trying to help Marti find her ticket. Even if Sierra had been there, they couldn't have gotten on the train without Marti's ticket. There seemed to be no reason for her to treat Alex so horribly. And because Marti had occasionally been nice to Alex, her rudeness seemed even worse; there was no telling when she would be nasty to him and when she would be sweet.

"I can carry something," Sierra offered.

"I can, too," Christy said.

Marti led the procession with stiff, angry steps. At the ticket counter, they had to wait in a line with six people ahead of them. Marti began to murmur about the lack of efficiency and the laziness of the workers. It was embarrassing to stand next to her. It took nearly 10 minutes for them to reach the clerk.

The whole time Sierra was replaying her risky jump in her mind. She had dreamed of a movielike romantic adieu with Alex. Instead she had leveled the poor guy and infuriated Marti. This day was not going according to plan.

"May I explain for you?" Alex asked Marti as they stepped up to the window. "If you think it would be helpful," he added hastily.

Too ruffled to show any more irritation, Marti clammed up again, so Alex took the opportunity to begin a swift explanation in German. The clerk answered in deep, rough German words. Alex was beginning to negotiate with him when an announcement came over the speaker system in German. This one sounded different from the destination announcements that were called out regularly.

Everyone in the station stopped to listen. Sierra noticed looks of surprise and annoyance appearing on faces.

"What are they saying?" Sierra whispered to Alex.

"All trains north have been canceled." He held up his finger to indicate he was still listening and she shouldn't speak.

"But we have to go north," Marti said. "That's all there is to it. How can they cancel all the trains north? What kind of country is this?"

Sierra watched Alex's face. Something stirred inside her. She bit her lower lip and watched Alex's body language.

His eyebrows rose slightly, then quickly plummeted. His lips formed a tiny "o," and he let out a slow stream of breath. People around the station began to murmur and then grew silent as they listened to the rest of the announcement. Alex squeezed his eyes shut and shook his head.

"It was your train," he said quietly. Then looking at Marti, Christy, and Sierra, he touched his fingers to Sierra's cheek. "The train you almost boarded went off the main track two kilometers from here. The rains weakened the ground. The mud went out under the track. They fear that many are dead."

"No," Sierra whispered.

Alex put one arm around her and one arm around

Christy, giving them a comforting hug. Then he went to Marti and put both arms around her, trying to hug her, but she wouldn't have it.

Pulling away from all of them, Marti looked wild-eyed at the news. "We could have all died," she said.

They stood silently, absorbing the thought. The clerk at the ticket counter spoke abruptly to Alex.

Alex raised a hand and said in English, "It does not matter now. *Danke.*"

He led the three dazed women over to an open spot on a bench and gathered their luggage around them. "Please. I have a phone call to make. Will you wait here a moment?"

"We're not going anywhere," Marti said numbly.

As soon as Alex walked away, Sierra began to make suggestions. "We could take a bus. Or maybe see about renting a car. What do you think?"

"I think we almost died," Marti said.

"I know you're not going to like my saying this, Aunt Marti," Christy said, "but can't you see what just happened? God protected us. Your lost ticket wasn't a bad thing. It was a God-thing. It kept us from boarding that train. Remember last night you said that if God is so loving and protective, then He would have to prove it to you? I think He just did."

This time, Marti didn't yell at Christy for spiritualizing yet another situation. Instead, a tear coursed down Marti's cheek. Then another and another. She reached into her purse to find a tissue.

Sierra felt all shivery inside. It was as though she had been invited to see a miracle—the melting of Marti's heart.

"Where's the rest room?" Marti asked, suddenly rising. Her face was pale.

"I saw it back there." Christy pointed toward the bathroom. "Do you want me to go with you?"

"If you would," Marti said, already heading in the direction Christy indicated.

Sierra watched the luggage and waited for Alex to return. He came back with a broad smile. "My cousin said it is okay."

"What's okay?"

"That I take his car. I will drive you to the airport."

"That's great, Alex," Sierra exclaimed, happy to spend more time with him. "You know it's a couple of hours' drive, though, don't you? Of course you do. That's really nice of you. Marti and Christy went to the rest room. They should be back in a minute."

"I can load the car. Or do you think I should wait for them?" Alex asked.

"I don't know. Maybe we should wait so we don't upset Marti."

"This is good," Alex said. "I had hoped for a chance to tell you how good it was for me to be with you. I think for my life always I will remember you, See-hair-a."

Suddenly, their tender good-bye moment had come. Sierra was too startled to know how to respond. This wasn't at all the way she had planned it.

"I wanted to say the same thing to you," Sierra said. She felt the pocket of her jeans to make sure her address was still there. Now that the opportunity had come, she felt shy about suggesting they write. Shyness was a new feeling for her.

Forcing herself to be vulnerable, Sierra reached over and touched Alex's arm. Earlier, she had planned to take his hand in hers, the way he had taken hers in the alcove, and then share her feelings with him. She had even hoped that he would have already taken her hand and told her his feelings. But he had spoken his heart without touching her, and now it felt clumsy trying to take his hand. Sierra gave Alex's arm a timid squeeze and let go.

"You have given me so much in these past few days, Alexander. I want you to know that your fervent love has opened up my passions."

He lifted an eyebrow slightly.

"Wait. That's not what I meant. You didn't hear that. What I meant was, you know, your verse. The one about loving each other fervently."

Before Sierra could explain further, a male voice boomed over the speakers. Alex listened intently and then interpreted. "They are arranging for passengers with tickets to take a bus. Would you then like to take the bus instead of my cousin's car?"

"We don't exactly have three tickets to cash in," Sierra said. "I think Marti would be more comfortable in the car."

"You are right. Please excuse. I go to check on parking

to make certain I have not exceeded the time."

Alex stepped away briskly, leaving Sierra by herself.

"That didn't go so well," she mumbled. *He probably thinks I'm wacky, telling him he opened up my passions. Boy, I sure haven't made things easy. First I knock him over, and then I scare him off. Father God, feel free to intervene at any time here.*

As soon as she thought it, Sierra felt terrible. God *had* intervened. He had gotten her off the train. Hundreds of other people hadn't gotten off, and now some of them were dead. Sierra's thoughts spun around. Finally, she was hit with the realization that she could have been dead right now.

Sierra was struck by the contrasting experiences she'd had these past few days. Life was absolutely wonderful, and life was absolutely horrible. Life was both.

Life was also a gift. God gave people life, and clearly He could also take it back any time He wanted.

He's God, Sierra reminded herself. *He can do whatever He wants.*

Chapter Eighteen

WHEN CHRISTY AND MARTI RETURNED FROM the rest room, Marti didn't look well at all. After a brief pause, Alex offered to drive them to the airport, and Marti accepted without flinching.

Sierra climbed into the car's backseat, feeling as though she were on borrowed time. She decided every moment of her life needed to count. God had kept her on this earth a little longer, and she wanted to make the most of the gift of life He had given her. She thought of the young couple she had seen saying good-bye at the train, and a lump formed in her throat. Was that young woman alive, or was she one of the train wreck's victims?

Turning her head, Sierra cried silently. The others in the car were quiet as well. Sierra's tears kept coming. The scenery along the way was a peaceful mix of green hills and fields of corn. She wondered how everything could look so calm and beautiful when something horrible had just happened. But she knew that often in life, there were no simple answers. Life was wonderful, and life was horrible. That was life.

These hard truths brought little comfort to Sierra as the car sped through one small town after another, each of them appearing like a village from a fairy tale. Most of the houses boasted small, tidy gardens packed with a variety of vegetables and bright flowers. The flashes of fresh color had a soothing effect on Sierra. But the sky continued to pout, threatening to rain its tears on them once more.

Marti rode with the front seat reclined and her hand on her forehead. Christy indicated silently that Marti had been sick to her stomach when they went to the bathroom in the train station. Sierra wondered if they would have to pull over along the way. She knew it was no fun to be sick when traveling, and she empathized with Marti. It didn't matter that Marti was probably sick from the combination of having too much wine the day before, along with being thrown into a nervous panic when they missed their train.

The narrow but well-paved road took them past a long, flat field where white sheep were grazing.

"Don't they look like big marshmallows on top of a birthday cake with green icing?" Sierra said.

"What are marshmallows?" Alex asked.

They were all keeping their voices low out of consideration for Marti. Alex's voice seemed loud even when he talked softly, though.

Sierra explained marshmallows, and Alex described a favorite treat from Russia. He explained it as a long white cube that sounded to Sierra like a stick of butter the size of a bread loaf.

"You eat wedges of butter all by themselves?"

"I know butter. This is not butter. It is much more of a delicacy." He described the treat and how it was made, trying to get Christy and Sierra to understand what it was like.

"That sounds like what we call lard," Christy said, wrinkling her nose. "We would never, and I do mean never, sit down to eat a slice of lard!"

"Pull over!" Marti shrieked.

Alex stopped the car alongside a grove of trees. Marti nearly tumbled from the car and got sick in the ditch that divided the road from the grove.

"Should I get out?" Christy asked.

"Did she want help when she was sick at the train station?" Sierra asked.

"No."

"Then she probably doesn't now either. Do you have tissue or anything?"

Christy reached for Marti's purse in the front seat and pulled out a travel packet of tissue.

"Are you okay?" Christy asked her aunt, handing her the packet.

"I'll be fine," Marti said. "As long as you can do me a favor and change your topic of conversation."

"Sorry," Christy said.

"Drive on, Alex," Marti said, adjusting her seat and rolling down her window. "We can't miss that plane."

"I'll need to stop for petrol at the next opportunity," he said.

"Fine, fine. I'll pay of course. Just drive faster."

They found a service station just before the entrance to the freeway, or autobahn, as Alex called it. Christy and Sierra went into the convenience store and bought Marti some water and mints. They also purchased drinks for themselves and Alex, some beef jerky, and a bag of cookies.

"It seems like a normal gas station in the States," Sierra said as they walked back to the car. "Except for the different brands of drinks and candy."

"And the prices," Christy said. "Do you realize the gas is more than twice what we pay?"

"I hope I remember that the next time I have to fill the car. I guess we don't appreciate a lot of things about life at home."

"That's for sure," Christy said as they settled back into the car. "I was thinking about how I'm going to get around here without a car. I guess I'll get used to the bus and train system. But it's going to be a whole new experience, trying to figure out everything."

"Thanks again for taking us to the airport," Sierra said, patting Alex on the back. He was pulling onto the autobahn and accelerating the car to keep up with the zooming traffic.

"How fast are we going?" Sierra asked.

"I don't know, but I remember hearing about these autobahns from a friend of mine, Alissa. She said people drove a hundred miles an hour, and I didn't believe her." Christy gave Sierra's leg a squeeze as Alex rapidly changed lanes. "I believe her now!"

They seemed to arrive at the airport in no time. The drive had definitely been faster than the train would have been.

Some of the color came back into Marti's face after they had checked in and were waiting for their flight.

"Are you feeling better?" Sierra asked.

"Yes, thank you." Marti reached into her purse. "Alex, thank you also. It appears you saved the day. Here's something for your trouble."

"It is not necessary," he said, holding up a hand to refuse Marti's money. "I wanted to do this for you."

"It was certainly kind of you. Thank you." Marti put back the money and glanced at her watch. "You should probably say your good-byes now. We'll be boarding in a few minutes."

Sierra had been wondering what would happen when this moment came. Would it be awkward to say good-bye to Alex in front of Christy and Marti? Should she try to explain to Alex what she meant earlier about her passions being awakened?

"Alexander," Christy said, stepping forward and shaking his hand warmly, "I'm so glad we met you that first day on the train. Thanks for everything."

"If I have another holiday here, perhaps I will see you at the school."

"I would love to see you again," Christy said.

Alex gave her a quick hug, kissing the air beside her cheeks—first the right side, then the left. Sierra had seen many Europeans greet each other in this way. She even had a friend from Italy, Antonio, who had kissed her on each cheek when he greeted her. He did that to all his female friends, so Sierra never considered it a kiss. Now, with the prospect of Alex saying good-bye to her in the same way, it suddenly seemed very much like a kiss.

He moved over to Aunt Marti and gave her the same warm gesture. She remained fixed in her rigid posture, but her expression was softer than it had been all day.

Now it was Sierra's turn. Her heart began to thump like a bongo drum, pulsing its rhythm to her throat. "Alex," she said in a low voice, leaning close so no one else could hear her, "I wanted to explain what I was trying to say before at the train station. You know, about your verse on loving others fervently. I don't think I know how to really love other people yet, but you do, and you showed me that kind of love by your living example. I'll never forget it. And I'll never forget you. I'm so glad I had the privilege of knowing you."

Sierra held her breath and replayed the words in her mind to see if she had been able to say what she meant. It was a little bumpy, but basically she had told Alex what she wanted to say. She smiled, satisfied.

Alex gave her a tender look, a look that gave her instant assurance he had heard her heart and understood what she meant. He leaned closer. His steady hand gently brushed a wisp of hair off her forehead.

Is he going to kiss me? Should I close my eyes? Maybe I had better leave them open. I could open one and close one. What am I thinking? I can't think straight! What should I do?

"*Meine Freunde,* I have in my heart," Alex said in his deep voice, "all these same thoughts for you. In heaven we will meet once again, and I will be glad for that day."

Sierra swallowed. "In heaven," she repeated. She knew he had called her "my friend" in German. Suddenly, she knew he wasn't going to kiss her. Not on the lips. And she knew Alex would never write to her either. Sierra's address remained in her pocket, but she knew Alex would remain in a tiny corner of her heart. And thankfully, Sierra had been able to tell him that.

"May the peace of Christ be upon you," Alex said.

"And upon you," Sierra repeated.

He leaned over, took her gently by both shoulders, and pressed his right cheek to hers. It felt cool against her blushing redness. She heard the sound of the kiss he sent into the air next to her ear. Then his head moved to her left cheek, and again, he kissed the air by her cheek.

Alex let go of Sierra's shoulders and, to her surprise, he put his right hand on his heart. Then Alex bowed to the three of them.

"May God be with all of you," he said with emotion.

Just then a female voice began to announce something in German.

"That must be for our flight," Marti said. "Come, girls."

Sierra and Christy followed Marti, and she handed the attendant their three tickets. Sierra turned to give Alex one last smile over her shoulder. Heaven could be a long time from now—or not. Either way, she wanted to remember that face until then.

Chapter Nineteen

T HE FLIGHT HOME WAS UNEVENTFUL. THAT, IN itself, was a welcome relief. When the trio deplaned in Los Angeles, Sierra said good-bye to Christy and Marti before catching the next flight to Portland. They were all so tired, it turned into a rather emotional scene.

"Thank you so much for inviting me, Marti," Sierra said. "I know some of the things I said and did were pretty annoying, and I apologize. I learned a lot on this trip, and I really appreciate your generosity and kindness in letting me come along. Thank you. I . . . " Sierra paused. "I love you."

Marti didn't look as startled as Sierra thought she would. But Sierra herself was startled to have those words even come to her mind.

"You were refreshing to have on the trip, Sierra," Marti said. She looked at Sierra with a fondness Sierra hadn't seen before. "I appreciate your loyalty to Christy. At first I didn't understand the friendship you two have. But, I must say, you are a good friend for my niece. A little too strong on the religious side, but then Christy seems attracted to your kind. Oh, and don't think I didn't notice your efforts to convert me." Marti included Christy in her sweeping gaze.

"I must admit, after they announced that our train had been derailed, I was almost persuaded to bow to your God. I'm sure it was from the stress of the moment and my sudden sickness. I do feel back to myself now."

Although Marti was acting extremely self-reliant, Sierra thought she detected a new tenderness in her eyes.

Christy and Sierra glanced at each other.

Oh, Marti, you are so close. Just stop fighting and surrender your life! Sierra thought. She could tell Christy was thinking the same thing.

"I'm going to miss you," Christy said, hugging Sierra.

"I'm going to miss you, too. Send me your address in Germany, and I'll definitely write."

They pulled away from each other, and both had tears streaming down their cheeks.

"And I'll write back," Christy said. "I promise."

"If you want to know what to buy for my birthday," Sierra said, wiping her tears with the back of her hand, "just send me one of those marzipan pastries from that little bakery."

"Okay," Christy laughed. "Should I send truffles for you, Aunt Marti?"

"No, dear, of course not. And don't you eat too many of them while you're there either."

Both girls laughed. Their eyes met again, locking in silent, eternal friendship.

"I love you—fervently," Sierra said.

Christy smiled. "And I love you fervently. Bye, Sierra."

They hugged again, and then Sierra got in line to board her flight to Portland. An hour and a half later, her parents met her as she got off the plane. They hugged and kissed her and listened to her chatter about everything all at once.

They were standing by the luggage carousel, waiting for Sierra's bag to come rolling around, when a flashback hit her. Last January, when she had returned from England, Paul had stood beside her at this very carousel, in nearly the same spot. He had thought she had his suitcase, but the luggage tag had proved it was hers.

Sierra remembered being judgmental of him on the flight home. Her approach had been to act grown up and witty, and her final words had been "Have a nice life."

Sierra closed her eyes, embarrassed now at the memory. Who was she trying to be? Where was the fervent love in that comment? She remembered how mature she had felt. After all, she had just traveled to England and back by herself.

Now that didn't seem like such a grand accomplishment. It was nothing compared with surviving a trip to Europe with Aunt Martha.

A loud buzzer sounded, and the luggage conveyor belt began its cycle.

Sierra remembered Paul's last words to her that day: "Don't ever change, Sierra."

I have changed, Paul. Something major has changed in my heart. I know now that it's not enough to have all the right answers and obey all the rules. If I don't have love, I'm nothing.

She wished she could tell that to Paul. If she ever had the chance, she decided she would apologize for her brash statements and the flippant letters she had sent him in the past. Not that it was likely she'd have the opportunity. The best she could do was learn from her experience and resolve to show love.

After all, she thought, *love is supposed to cover a multitude of sins. Does that include a multitude of immature blunders?*

"This one is yours, isn't it?" her dad asked, reaching for Sierra's luggage.

"Yes," Sierra responded, returning to the present. "That one's mine."

When they got home, Sierra hugged her little brothers, kissed Granna Mae, and chatted with her family for nearly an hour.

"Did you bring us anything?" Gavin asked.

Sierra felt bad. She hadn't been looking for souvenirs when she had shopped with Marti. "I think I have some German greeting cards. They're a little bent but kind of funny. I didn't really shop for souvenirs. The only thing I bought was some tea. I'll bring some stuff next time."

"You're going again?" Dillon asked.

"I might. Does anybody want some jasmine spice tea?"

Sierra had no takers, so she made a steaming cup for herself. Then, saying good night, she went up to her room to crash, even though it was still light outside.

"I think you'll like the surprise you're going to find up

there," Mrs. Jensen said as Sierra climbed the stairs. But she didn't care what the surprise was. All she wanted to do was reacquaint herself with her fluffy pillow.

Sierra opened the door to a tidy room. Her mom must have gotten fed up with the clutter while Sierra was gone. The window was open, letting in a warm summer breeze. With all the mess cleared away, Sierra immediately noticed a piece of paper on top of her neatly made bed. The paper had been all crumpled but was now smoothed out. It was a letter to her with no envelope. The distinctive handwriting was in black ink, written in a mixture of printing and cursive.

"Paul," Sierra whispered into the air.

Snatching up the letter, Sierra eagerly read "Dear Daffodil Queen."

Wait a minute, Sierra thought.

She scanned the letter and checked the signature. It was a letter from Paul, all right. But it was one he had written last spring. Sierra had been so frustrated with him, she had wadded it up and tossed it into the trash. Obviously, it had never made it to the city dump. It probably was lost behind her dresser or something until her mom found it while cleaning her room.

Sierra didn't mind that her mother had probably read it. It was a dopey letter anyhow. In a way she was glad her mom had found it. Sierra had one other letter from Paul, which he had written right after they had met. That one she had saved in the top drawer of her antique dresser.

Smoothing the wrinkles in this lost-and-found letter,

Sierra carried it over to the dresser to tuck into the top drawer with her other letter. She glanced into the antique oval mirror to see how scruffy she looked from the long trip home. But instead of her own reflection, Sierra saw an envelope wedged into the right-hand, bottom corner of the mirror. It was addressed to her, and the return address was Scotland. And, most important, the letter was written in familiar bold black ink.

Her hand began to shake as she reached for it. As a child, Sierra's favorite adventure was having treasure hunts. On many birthdays and Christmases, her mother had written clever clues that had led Sierra all over the house and yard in search of her gift. It made her smile to think her mom probably had to clean her room just for the chance to place the "clue" letter, which would lead Sierra to the dresser drawer, where she would notice the mirror and the new letter. Sierra might never have found it otherwise.

With this newest correspondence in her hand, Sierra floated to the overstuffed chair by the window. It felt strange not to have to move the usual pile of clothes as she lowered herself into the chair. With her thumbnail, Sierra slit open the envelope and slowly took out the page of ivory parchment.

> *Dear Sierra,*
> *This may come as a complete shock that I am writing you. I have to admit, it's a little surprising to me. Something has been very much on my mind*

since I left Portland in June. That something is you.

The night before I left for Scotland, I went to your house for dinner as a favor to my brother. Ever since he had started to date your sister, Jeremy had wanted me to have a meal with Tawni's family and "be nice" to you. I fulfilled my promise to him and even took you out to coffee. To me, it was nothing more than a favor.

What I didn't count on was the way you got to me, Sierra. As I think about it even now, I feel something I have never felt before. You said something about God having His mark on me, and that He's going to do something with my life. I believe He already has done something. He's brought me here, to the land of my kin. Spiritually, it's a dark place where so many people are without hope. But in the short time I've been here, I've come alive.

I know God, Sierra. It's different from knowing about Him. I talk to Him all the time. I go for long walks in the highlands, and I sing out loud to Him. I can't believe I'm telling you this, except somehow I feel as if you, of all the people I know, will understand what's going on in my life.

How did you know God had "marked" me? Why did you pray for me all those months, like you said? Where does your zeal come from, Sierra? For the first time in my life, I'm beginning to desire the same things.

I don't know if any of this makes sense to you. If you don't want to write back, believe me, I'll under-

stand. But I'd like to ask you if you would start a correspondence with me. I'm not sure that you and I got off to the best start when we met in England. I think I was a different person then. Do you believe in second chances? I'd like a second chance at our relationship.

It's with great pleasure that I can tell you this. . . . I've been praying for you, Sierra. And I will continue to, whether you write to me or not.

Sincerely yours,
Paul

Sierra read the letter again—slowly this time, moving her lips. It was sweeter the second time. And after the fourth time, she felt overwhelmed by tears. She blinked them back and read it a fifth time.

Paul is praying for me. I'll have to tell him about the train and about Alex, and I wonder if Jeremy told him about Doug and Tracy's wedding? Oh, and the Highland House. He's going to want to hear how things are going at the homeless shelter his uncle runs. There's so much to tell him.

Her mind raced with all the possible things she could write to him about. The words lined up inside her head and began to multiply until they smashed together in her jet-lagged mind.

I can't write anything until I sleep.

Going over to her bed, Sierra folded the treasured letter and placed it under her pillow. Kicking off her shoes, she curled up in her inviting bed. Exhaustion pulled its invisible blanket over her and passed a dark hand over her heavy eyelids. A contented smile curved across her lips.

She might not know exactly how to enter into this wonderful, new relationship with Paul, but Sierra definitely knew she was ready to open her heart.

Don't Miss the Captivating Stories in the Sierra Jensen Series

With This Ring (#6)

Sierra couldn't be happier when she goes to Southern California to join Christy Miller and their friends at the wedding they've all been waiting for. Amid the "I dos" and Tracy and Doug's first kiss ever, Sierra realizes that purity is truly sacred and something worth having! Can she convince her friend Amy of the same thing?

Without a Doubt (#5)

When Drake—the gorgeous guy Amy likes—reveals his interest in Sierra, life gets complicated. Sierra wonders if she can trust her emotions. And when a freak snowstorm hits during a backpacking trip with her youth group, she is forced to face her doubts. Will Sierra turn to God to help her sort things out?

Close Your Eyes (#4)

Sparks fly when Sierra runs into Paul while volunteering at a shelter. But the situation gets sticky when Paul comes over for dinner and Randy shows up at the same time! Will Sierra learn to trust God for guidance in her feelings for Randy and Paul?

Don't You Wish (#3)

Sierra is excited about visiting Christy Miller in California during Easter break. She's ready to relax and leave her troubles behind. Unfortunately, a nagging "trouble" has followed her there—her sister, Tawni! Somehow, Tawni seems to win the attention of everyone . . . even a guy. Surrounded by couples, can Sierra learn to be content alone?

In Your Dreams (#2)

Sierra's junior year is nothing like she dreamed. With no job, no friends, a sick grandmother, and a neat-freak sister, her life is becoming a nightmare! And just when things start to go her way—she even gets asked out on a date—Sierra runs into Paul. How can she get him out of her head if he keeps showing up?

Only You, Sierra (#1)

During Sierra's weeklong missions trip in Europe, her family moves to a different state. Returning home, she dreads the loneliness of going to a new high school—until she meets Paul in the airport. Will she ever see this mystery man again?

Available at your favorite Christian bookstore.

Get to Know Sierra's Friend Christy Miller!

Twelve romantic adventures are just waiting to be discovered in the smash-hit "Christy Miller Series." Each captivating story tells of Christy's struggle to stick by her convictions and trust in God's timing.

A Promise Is Forever
On a European trip with her friends, Christy finds it difficult to keep her mind off Todd. Will God ever bring them back together?

Sweet Dreams
Christy's dreams become reality when Todd finally opens his heart to her. But her relationship with her best friend goes downhill fast when Katie starts dating a non-Christian.

A Time to Cherish
A surprise houseboat trip! Her senior year! Lots of friends! Life couldn't be better for Christy until . . .

Seventeen Wishes
Christy is off to summer camp—as a counselor for a cabin of wild fifth-grade girls.

Starry Night
Christy is torn between going to the Rose Bowl Parade with her friends or on a surprise vacation with her family.

True Friends
Christy sets out with the ski club and discovers the group is thinking of doing something more than hitting the slopes.

A Heart Full of Hope
A dazzling dream date, a jammin' job, a cool car. And lots of freedom! Christy has it all. Or does she?

Island Dreamer
It's an incredible tropical adventure when Christy celebrates her sixteenth birthday on Maui.

Surprise Endings
Christy tries out for cheerleader, learns a classmate is out to get her, and schedules two dates for the same night.

Yours Forever
Fifteen-year-old Christy does everything in her power to win Todd's attention.

A Whisper and a Wish
Christy is convinced that dreams do come true when her family moves to California and the cutest guy in school shows an interest in her.

Summer Promise
Christy spends the summer at the beach with her wealthy aunt and uncle. Will she do something she'll later regret?

Available at your favorite Christian bookstore.